THE IRRESISTIBLE MISS PEPPIWELL

Scandalous House of Calydon

THE IRRESISTIBLE MISS PEPPIWELL

Scandalous House of Calydon

STACY REID

This book is a work of fiction. Names, characters, places, and incidents are the product of the author's imagination or are used fictitiously. Any resemblance to actual events, locales, or persons, living or dead, is coincidental.

Copyright © 2014 by Stacy Reid. All rights reserved, including the right to reproduce, distribute, or transmit in any form or by any means. For information regarding subsidiary rights, please contact the Publisher.

Entangled Publishing, LLC
2614 South Timberline Road
Suite 109
Fort Collins, CO 80525
Visit our website at www.entangledpublishing.com.

Scandalous is an imprint of Entangled Publishing, LLC.

Edited by Nina Bruhns
Cover design by Erin Dameron-Hill
Cover art from Period Images, iStock, and Shutterstock

Manufactured in the United States of America

First Edition August 2014

SCANDALOUS

For my love, Dusean Nelson.

Chapter One

LONDON OCTOBER 1882

The Honorable Lord Anthony Thornton had never before seen such vivid golden-red hair. It shone iridescently under the candlelight of the crystal chandeliers in the glittering ballroom, the glorious hue of sunset. It belonged to a stunning jewel standing aloof amongst the dandies who were fluttering about vying for her attention, a cold, serene beauty. The lady was magnificent, with elegant carriage, fine cheekbones, slightly slanted eyes, and the most exotic full lips Anthony had ever seen.

His gaze traced the graceful length of her throat down to the gentle swell of her breasts, encircled her tiny waist, curved out toward hips that flared enticingly. As he moved to approach her, he realized why she stood out from all the other women. It was not her startling beauty. There were, indeed, more dazzling women laughing and twirling, soaking up the decadence of the ballroom, titillated by the vociferous nature of society that could chew them up like the sleeping monster it was.

No. It was her eyes. They stared blankly, devoid of enjoyment. Her lips curved in a smile of pure frost as she accepted a glass of punch from one of her many admirers. They seemed anxious to please her, though she remained uncaring.

Waylaid by his host, Anthony paused without taking his gaze from her.

"It seems the ice maiden has made another conquest," Jason Fullerton, the Earl of Calvert, murmured.

Anthony finally shifted his focus from her and met the eyes of his friend. Humor kicked up the corners of Calvert's lips, twitching his moustache.

"Ice maiden?" Anthony queried.

"Colder than the Arctic itself, enough to freeze a man's vitals with thought alone. The fops are wasting their time. She has not deigned to show favor to anyone, and I, for one, am puzzled, since she has nothing to tempt a man with, save her fortune."

Anthony thought Jason wrong as he watched her tuck away a tendril that teased her forehead. The raising of her arm stretched her gown across her breasts. Her cool feminine sensuality lured him. He did not think it deliberate, the way she arched her neck as she captured another loose wisp and tucked it behind her ear.

Her hair was pinned in some sort of knot, with tendrils cascading in loose spirals down to kiss her shoulders. The cut of her ball gown was mouthwateringly exquisite. The deep blue silken dress clung alluringly to her frame, hugging her curves. It bared the creamy expanse of her shoulders and drew his eyes to her barely there décolletage. His gaze lingered over the gentle swell of her breasts. She was not full-figured by any means, her silhouette more subtle and elegant. He decided the most glorious thing about the ice beauty was her hair, and he tried not to focus too much on the lush ripeness of her lips. She really had the most inviting mouth.

"Introduce us," Anthony quietly demanded.

"Are you foxed?" Calvert retorted. "I was sure you were here for Lady Galveston. The *on dit* is that you are searching for a new mistress."

Anthony ignored the laughter that taunted him from Calvert's pale blue eyes. But on that point, the earl was correct. Anthony had attended the ball because he sought a distraction with whom he could sate himself. He wished to leave the cares of the world behind for the night—but he did not seek it from a new mistress.

"Look at the delightful curves of Lady Galveston," Calvert urged. "She, my friend, is where your efforts would be more productively directed."

He dismissed the earl's sly whisper and stalked toward the ice beauty. He ignored those who tried to capture his attention, moving through the crowded ballroom without pause. As he drew closer he noted her eyes were golden brown, amber liquid with cold flashes of gold, the color of chilled Irish whiskey. They lingered on him for a moment and then flicked away dismissively.

He was intrigued.

He knew the effect his face normally had on debutantes and women of society. The married ones issued fawning salacious propositions, while the virginal misses behaved like complete swooning nitwits. He hated it, and did everything in his power to make his appearance more severe. He'd actually been well pleased with the scar over his left eyebrow he had recently been dealt from boxing.

"I am telling you, she will unman you with a mere glance," Calvert drawled, strolling along beside him.

Anthony did not acknowledge the earl's crude chuckle as they stopped in front of her. She glanced at them, her mien unreadable. She had freckles. They dashed over her nose and sprinkled her cheeks.

"Miss Peppiwell, may I present, Lord Anthony Thornton."

She dipped into a shallow curtsy. "My lord." Her murmur was flat, uninterested.

After making his swift introductions, Calvert departed with a smirk on his lips.

With a single imperious glance from Anthony, the dandies fluttering around her faded into the glittering crowd. From the cool arch of her brows, he surmised she noticed.

"May I have the next dance on your card, Miss Peppiwell?"

"I do not dance." She pronounced her vowels with a lilt, and her voice was husky with a musical twang. American. From Boston, if he was not mistaken.

He was undaunted by her aloofness. Instead, interest stirred within. It had been weeks since he'd felt desire for any woman. "If not a dance, will you honor me with a twirl in the garden?"

"It seems I have caught the attention of the bored and dissolute Lord Anthony." Her sonorous voice washed over him. She did not sound pleased.

"Dissolute? You wound me."

"So you admit to being bored and seeking out the ice princess?" She stared at him chillingly.

He tipped his head as he slowly regarded her. The buzz of the room faded, and he met her gaze without expression. He concluded she could beat him at poker, though he was revered for his game play. "I sought out a lady for a dance, that is all."

"I am not a lady. I do not hold the lofty title you desire. Will you still want a dance if I am only a miss?" Her lips pursed as she stared at him with something akin to acerbity.

"Ah, I see the dilemma now. You are judging me unjustly." He was gratified to see her spine snap taut. He had begun to think her a sculpture.

"I have done nothing of the sort."

"It was you, Miss Peppiwell, who deemed a woman can only be a lady by virtue of a title, and that I would have a similar opinion."

She flushed, and he gritted his teeth in chagrin as arousal teased at him, hardening his length. He was at a bloody ball, hardly the place to be stirred even slightly.

"I concede, sir, I have been rude. Please accept my apologies." She gracefully bowed her head, then smiled at him.

Though she sounded sincere her smile did not quite reach her eyes. They remained distant. The flush in her cheeks had already receded, giving her that cold look once more. He did not like it. He should not have cared, having only just met the chit, but he preferred her with the heat that colored her skin and quickened the pulse at her throat. He found it curious that she was aware of the gossip about her. Most young ladies remained oblivious until the cruel jaws of society devoured them.

He made another stab at eliciting a reaction from her. "My lord," he stated.

"I beg your pardon?"

"You referred to me as 'sir.' The proper mode of address is 'my lord,' or 'Lord Anthony.'"

Anger flared in her eyes. They shot sparks, which dampened immediately as if they had been doused with the chilliest of waters. He was riveted. She opened her mouth as if to form a scathing reply, but froze. He had not thought her capable of an even deeper stillness. And yet, a look of panic chased across her features before she slammed the shutters down completely. He turned with an air of casual indifference, curious to know who had the ability to induce panic in this paragon of indifference.

"Lord Anthony." The grating voice of Lord Orwell trumpeted, and Anthony dipped his head in acknowledgement. He smoothed his features into polite blankness, noting the salacious leer Orwell directed at Miss Peppiwell.

"My dear, I trust you saved a dance for me," Orwell said. His smile was so toadying that it sickened Anthony. As a waltz started, Orwell held out his arm, clearly expecting her obedience.

"I fear, Lord Orwell, I promised Lord Anthony the last dance on my card." She subtly shifted closer to Anthony.

A smile curved his lips at the slight inflection of disdain in her pronunciation of their titles.

"I insist I have this dance, Phillipa," Orwell snapped.

Anthony found it curious that the lady did not correct Orwell's intimate use of her name. However, she drew herself more upright and seemed to generate a deeper chill around her. Anthony's chuckle drew the other man's gaze.

He looked arrogantly down his nose at Orwell's shorter, stockier frame. "As you see, I have the honor of escorting Miss Peppiwell."

"Are you still here?" Orwell said, genuinely surprised.

Anthony went stiff with anger, and Orwell flushed, belatedly registering his error. "Thornton…I had not realized." He fidgeted with his cravat as if feeling a noose tightening around his neck.

Anthony's intrigue deepened. Orwell had been so obsessed with the sensual Miss Peppiwell, it seemed that he had no issue being rude and dismissive, forgetting Anthony was the financial genius behind the Calydon Holdings. His brother might be the Duke of Calydon, but Anthony's financial power was so vast he could crush a man with a mere lift of his brow.

The cords of a waltz struck up. Anthony inclined his head in scant acknowledgment as he led Miss Peppiwell onto the dance floor, sweeping her into the rousing steps. A tingle of unease stirred through him at the avaricious way Orwell stared after them. Something glittered in his gaze—malice tinged with greed and obvious lust.

Anthony glanced down at her as she stared stonily at his shoulder. "Orwell is not a man any young lady should be involved with."

"I did not ask, nor do I require, your remonstrance." There was a slight pause and then a gusty expulsion that surprised him. "However, I thank you for going along with my ruse."

"A small thing to have you in my arms."

"It is futile to try your wiles on me, Lord Anthony. I am immune to such devices." The watchful frostiness had returned.

"I have no desire to try wiles or anything else on you," he said in a deliberately disinterested tone.

"So your reputation as one of the most licentious rakes in society is false, I presume?"

"Undeserved, I assure you." He twirled, spinning her with graceful ease around the dance floor. "I do not prey on the innocent."

He felt the slight stiffening of her body and he followed the lashes that swooped down obscuring her eyes. He was not sure, but he thought he had seen a flare of anger. Interesting.

"And yet, here you are." The affront in her tone was unmistakable. "Have you presumed to refer to me as impure?"

"As I am not preying on you, the matter of your innocence is moot."

The longest of lashes flickered, and she peered up at him. He wished there was some nuance of expression to give an inkling of her thoughts. His gaze slashed to Orwell, who waited, foot tapping impatiently at the edge of the dance floor. She glanced to Orwell as Anthony spun her past in a swirl and he assessed the flash of distaste in her expression.

"I fear you will not be able to refuse him without causing some gossip. He appears most insistent."

She directed her scorn toward Anthony. He was not sure which he preferred, the coldness or the disdain.

"I desire to avoid a lecher from pawing at me, yet to do so, your polite society would deem I am behaving inappropriately."

"Society is fickle, indeed. However, if you wish for his attentions to be directed elsewhere, I will see to it."

He was pleased to note that she could not disguise her surprise. Her eyes widened, and their dark gold glittered. "And why would you render such assistance to someone you do not know? Or about a situation you do not comprehend?" she asked, sounding genuinely curious.

He shrugged, then spun her into several dizzying spins before replying, "I have been accused of being gentlemanly several times. It might be that my duty was drilled into me from birth to respond to a damsel in distress."

Her chin tilted haughtily, and he found himself counting the freckles on her nose. She had eleven.

"I am not in distress, and I am certainly not a damsel."

He smiled, titillated by her hauteur. "Nevertheless, my offer stands."

"How kind of you," she said acidly. "And how would you achieve such a feat? A duel, perhaps, like our forefathers? Pistols at dawn?"

"The mere sign of my displeasure would be sufficient," he stated ignoring her sarcasm.

"It must be convenient to have your impeccable bloodlines and be as rich as Croesus. It must make you feel like a king among people whom you deem lower than yourself."

"You have not been acquainted with me long enough to classify me as either boorish or arrogant as you suggest, Miss Peppiwell."

Full, pouty lips thinned, and she lowered her gaze. "You are correct, my lord. Forgive me." She appeared genuinely chastened.

He studied her assessingly. Up close, he couldn't call her beautiful in the classical sense. Yet, he felt a definite niggle of need tightening inside him. He had not been involved with his mistress for several weeks now, having committed himself to the pursuit of a proper wife. He had a lady in mind, but she resided in the country and it wasn't exactly working out as he'd hoped. Restless and edgy, he had decided to attend Lady Calvert's midnight ball, wanting a distraction.

By all rights, he should be concentrating on the stunning widow Lady Galveston, who had been throwing him sultry looks since his arrival, but he had to admit the slender redhead with her cold, golden eyes interested him far more. Well, she had at least made his cock stir for the first time in ages.

"Orwell is trying to find you in the crowd. I am taller than most, so he will find us shortly," he observed.

Her lips parted as he whirled her several paces away, out of Orwell's view. "The oaf is distressingly persistent," she agreed.

Anthony watched Orwell slicing through the crowd, almost frantic in his attempt to keep Miss Peppiwell in his sight.

"Shall I rescue you?" Anthony questioned, twirling her with powerful movements.

"A crushing of his ego or wealth is not necessary. If you could deposit me in the library, I will be fine."

Anthony wasted no time deftly whisking her through the throng and down the corridor to the library on the first floor. He hesitated briefly, then ushered her inside.

She withdrew and turned a pointed gaze on him that again had gone arctic. "I thank you, Lord Anthony, and I bid you good night."

He scanned the room, spying a game of chess resting on a massive oak desk. "Do you play?" He indicated the chessboard as he sauntered toward the drinks table to pour sherry into two glasses.

"I had planned on reading, my lord. I am familiar with Lady Prescott's library and there is a particular book of Henry James I am eager to read."

He smiled, as at last some sort of animation entered her features. "Ah."

"I suppose you are repulsed by females who engage in intellectual discourse, as Lord Hoyt so thoughtfully enlightened me earlier?" The curve of her lips was sardonic.

"Of course not. A woman who reads has much to recommend her." He frowned, observing the deep wariness that darkened her gaze.

With a single glance, she dismissed him.

He'd never had a female show such immunity to his physique. He fleetingly wondered if her attractions lay with the same sex. It was not vanity, more an awareness of his own sensuality. "Are you deliberately trying to be elusive?"

"Me?" She blinked at him rapidly, the only sign of her surprise. "On the contrary, I am not interested in your charms. I am actually trying to be rid of you."

His laughter seemed to bemuse her. "Are all Boston ladies as candid as you are?" he asked, appreciating the forthrightness of speech that had not been wrapped in innuendo or sweet evasiveness.

"Shouldn't I be? I suppose I must acclimate myself to the idea that honesty is frowned upon," she retorted, her steady gaze challenging him.

He liked it. And was gratified that his guess as to her hometown had proved correct.

"In that case, Miss Peppiwell..." He downed his drink in a single swallow, sauntered forward and lifted her hand, brushing his lips fleetingly over it. He wished the glove did not separate her skin from his.

She graced him with one of those smiles that did not reach her eyes. "Good evening, sir…Lord Anthony."

He did not release her hand. Some temptations should not be resisted.

With that thought, he dipped his head and captured her lips. He told himself he only did it to see if she could be rattled, but knew it for a lie. The berry ripeness of her lips had been tantalizing him since he first saw them.

He drew her closer and pillowed her breasts to his chest.

He chuckled against the lips she pressed together so primly, but he was not disappointed, for the contours of those lips were soft and luscious. He lifted his head slowly, and smiled at what he saw. No affront, not even a slap to his cheek for his audacity. Just an aloofness and condescending hauteur as she looked down her nose at him, despite the fact he stood much taller. But behind her studied iciness, he swore he detected a spark of heat, a curl of unwilling want in those amber eyes.

His intrigue deepened. He did not believe he had to look any closer.

It was quite possible he had found his future bride in the ice maiden.

...

The Honorable Lord Anthony Thornton was dangerous. His touch evoked an unbidden need Phillipa did not want.

She held herself perfectly still, blanking her mind. His head dipped, bringing his sensual lips down once more to tease hers. Heat rose within her, but Phillipa buried it under hated memories of the cruel taunts and painful grasping of her nemesis.

Lord Anthony's lips, however, roamed over her warmly, firm and alluring. She repressed a moan that tried to escape. She could not, would not, give him an inkling of the sharp desire that slashed through her body at his touch.

He caressed her lips with a flick of his tongue, and then his soft chuckle vibrated to the core of her. He lifted his head, his lips quirked, and she fought to maintain an air of casual indifference. *The bloody scoundrel!* "Are you quite finished, my lord?"

"Indeed. I bid you good night, Miss Peppiwell. It was a pleasure dancing with you. Enjoy your reading."

"Good evening, Lord Anthony." She kept her features schooled and her feet rooted to the spot as he sauntered out of the library. She did not think his walk one of arrogance, more of inborn confidence. The library door closed with a *snick*, and befitting the lack of an audience, she wilted.

A gusty breath expelled from her lungs, and she rotated her shoulders, working the tightness out of them. Her heart still thumped and arousal teased her flesh. She snorted, disgusted with herself. At the first sign of a pretty face, her resolve, hardened by painful experiences, had cracked.

The man unsettled her. She stalked toward the bookshelf with anger in her step. She let her fingers fly with nimble speed over the titles until she found a copy of *The Portrait of a Lady*. She swallowed and dropped her forehead onto the cool wood of the bookshelf. She was lying to herself, and she hated that. She prided herself on being forthright with her thoughts and actions.

Lord Anthony was certainly not the only attractive man she had encountered since her launch into London society. Lord Orwell, the slimy blackguard, had a pleasant face that hid his vulgar crudity. Then there was Lord Hoyt, the handsome viscount who pursued her relentlessly, more for her fortune than anything else. Yet, Lord Anthony had been the only one to cause her protective wall to tremble.

A ripple in the crowd had alerted her to his presence when he first approached her, and she had assessed him out of curiosity. She'd deduced from the whispers that swept through the room, that he had not been expected to make an appearance. *And* he was a Thornton, a member of the scandalous house of Calydon. He was one of *them*—a privileged lord—brother to one of the most powerful dukes in the realm. She supposed that should have told her everything.

It certainly explained his arrogance in kissing her within minutes of their first introduction.

She was used to beautiful men. But she hated that simply from his prowl across the room, she had felt that low tug, that slow pooling of heat between her legs, with an intensity she'd never felt before. He was powerfully built, and even though she was tall in comparison to the dainty beauties of London society, she had felt dwarfed as he loomed over her in their dance.

He seemed darkly delicious, though it confounded her why. After all, his locks were golden, his eyes green, and his face the most stunningly handsome she had ever beheld. She had been greatly relieved to see the scar above his eye, branding him as human, after all, and not some fallen angel. Beauty alone had never attracted her, but he appealed to a degree she found staggering.

The doorknob rattled, and she snapped her head up. She tensed as she waited for someone to intrude. She hated attending these events, but her mother, her dear sister, Payton, and her aunt, the Countess of Merryweather, lived for the social whirl. Phillipa could hardly protest, not wishing to reveal the depth of her dislike for Orwell. Thankfully, the year was drawing to a close, so they only attended a few balls. The majority of the *haute monde* had already retired to the country.

She hurried to the door and latched it when no one entered, then sauntered to the sofa closest to the fireplace. She threw herself, without any semblance of ladylike decorum, into its depth, smirking at the simple indulgence of not sitting like a priggish miss.

Unbidden, her mind skipped to Lord Anthony. Thoughts of his lips and how good they'd felt on hers had her grinding her teeth. Oh, how she had wanted to sink into the kiss and accept the pleasure that he could give! A swift feeling of shame arose and she ruthlessly buried the heat that tried to flush her cheeks, ensconcing it under the coldness she used to protect herself.

It would be a grave mistake to trust another nobleman.

An unwanted shimmer of excitement pulsed through her, and her heart thumped in dismay at the thought of ever encountering him again. He roused feelings in her that she did not want to indulge in. Her mind shifted to Lord Orwell and her mouth turned down in distaste. *The lecherous bastard.* For all she knew, Lord Anthony was just like Orwell.

She gave a snort of repugnance as she snapped open James's masterpiece, refusing to waste another moment thinking about a certain green-eyed lord.

Chapter Two

Two days later, the cold country air stung Anthony's lungs, but did not prevent him from enjoying his morning ride with the beautiful Lady Jocelyn. He'd stopped off at his newly acquired Baybrook property, as had become his habit of the last few weeks, on his way to Sherring Cross, his brother, the Duke of Calydon's ancestral estate. Apparently a letter had arrived for him from their solicitor, which Sebastian wished to discuss.

Anthony had welcomed the distraction. For an endless day and two long nights the intriguing Miss Phillipa Peppiwell had been haunting his thoughts and heating his dreams. He had specifically decided on this morning's detour…a valiant attempt to put her from his mind.

It wasn't working.

A gray mare thundered past him. Raven tresses and joyous laughter from Lady Jocelyn rode the wind, charming him with the lady's fiery, yet pleasing disposition. Unlike a certain ice maiden he could name.

"You are too slow, Lord Anthony," she said with a chortle.

She spun her mare around gracefully and cantered toward him. "I win."

He banished the image of whiskey eyes and glorious red hair and turned a smile toward Lady Jocelyn. To his mild annoyance, her appearance did not lance arousal through him. Her dark beauty put her among the most stunning women he'd ever seen, yet the most feeling she excited in him was simple appreciation. He was content to look, but not tempted to taste. Especially after his titillating encounter with the coolly sensual Miss Peppiwell.

Lady Jocelyn had appeared out of nowhere, so different from the other young ladies of the *haute monde*, and he had been captivated by her fiery personality. He'd thought it a pity she had not been presented for her season, for she would have either shocked or charmed society. They had been distantly acquainted for some years, since her family was friendly with Lord Calvert's brood, whom he visited regularly at their countryseat. However, Anthony's new property bordered Stonehaven, her father's estate, and they had become much closer friends over the past several weeks. It was probably a little late to realize he was not drawn to Lady Jocelyn in the way he had hoped. He had been courting her for a couple of weeks now. Riding up from London to his new estate to oversee the renovations, he'd stolen kisses that hadn't roused him, and had escorted her to country balls and picnics.

She was a whirlwind, her energy and vivacity unrelenting. He knew she wanted marriage for the same reason many of the ladies of society did. Money. Which suited him fine—it was the usual way of things. If only they'd been more attracted, then at least it could possibly grow to love.

She did not, it seemed, hunger for his touch, either. She barely responded to his kisses, her lips pursed primly, no doubt thinking that was all to it. He had shocked himself by not pressing for deeper tastes. He simply hadn't had the desire.

"What are you thinking about when you gaze so far away?" she asked him.

He chuckled, finding her lack of artifice refreshing. What was it about him and unrefined misses? "Investments," he answered, since his actual thoughts were inappropriate.

"Indeed?" She gave him a dubious frown. "Is that a potential investment you hold in your hand?"

He glanced at the golden locket dangling from his fingers. Ice settled into his gut and he exhaled, releasing the tension from his body. He didn't *have* to decide today. "In a way. It was a gift from my brother, the Duke of Calydon."

"An unusual gift between brothers." She leaned over her pommel, reaching for it. He handed it to her, watching her examine its filigree and delicate chain. "It's very beautiful."

"It belonged to our mother's family. It is supposed to be handed down to the wife of the firstborn son in the family."

She smiled. "What a lovely tradition."

"As you may know, Calydon refuses to marry, so he gifted it to me to present to my wife."

Her gray eyes widened, and the surge of hope in her gaze made his gut clench. Her fingers tightened on the locket, and her gaze swept over to her father's lands. He knew without looking what she saw—fields and tenant houses in desperate need of funding.

Her eyes slashed back to his, before reaching out to hand him back the locket.

"Keep it," he said on impulse.

"What are you saying?" Lady Jocelyn asked slowly.

"I want you to hold onto it for me."

"You would trust me with such a family treasure?"

"Why not? Are we not friends?" She gave him a blinding smile, punching him with her beauty.

He tried again to summon a spark of desire for her, and failed. He gritted his teeth in anger. He was thinking she would make him a good companion, but damn it to hell, he should feel something beyond warm affection and appreciation of his wife's beauty.

He made the decision to return to London the following day. A deep part of him wanted to explore the attraction he felt for the sensual Miss Peppiwell.

He should try to concentrate on the woman in front of him. Lady Jocelyn was a lady, through and through. Her lineage was a noble one. She understood her role in London's *haute monde*. She wanted to get married and have children, as befitted her position—he had known it from the minute she greeted him upon their reacquaintance, betraying a look of assessing him as a potential suitor.

In other words, she was the perfect woman to take as wife.

It was a damned shame he had no desire to do so.

Chapter Three

He was a bastard.

A fist slammed into Anthony's side, sharp and wicked. His body jerked under the power of the punch, and he welcomed the bite of pain. He bobbed and weaved, rolling with graceful speed as he danced around his boxing partner, his brother Sebastian.

Or should he say his half brother?

Anthony felt the crack of leather on flesh and blanked his mind, refusing to allow the fury that powered through him to hold sway. Instead, he moved in to deliver rapid-fire punches at Sebastian. The edge of something dark licked at his insides, trying to fray his control. He held onto it with a cold determination he had not thought himself capable of before now.

"Mayhap, boxing is not the best way to relieve your tension." The wry murmur of his brother's voice drew him from the black emotions that wanted to pull him under.

He met Sebastian's blue gaze and wiped all thoughts from his face. He did not need the concern that he saw shadowing his brother's eyes. "I am not tense." He unwrapped his hand, looking at the raw knuckles. They did not wear boxing gloves; their only concession to protecting their flesh was a binding of soft leather.

"Did you not read the letter from Newport?" Sebastian queried.

Newport was Anthony's solicitor, and the last thing he wanted to talk about was the damn letter he had received from him. Anthony grabbed the towel Sebastian held out and raked it over his skin with a curse. "I did."

"Then you are tense, brother. Why don't you go and see Georgina?"

He tried to conjure up images of his former mistress, but he only saw sensual lips and whiskey-colored eyes in a freckled face. He shook his head sharply, not welcoming the reminder of Miss Peppiwell. "I bid Georgina adieu with a few generous gifts."

Sebastian threw him a startled look. "Why? I thought her experienced enough to suit your tastes."

"I grew bored."

"Were you not fond of her?"

Anthony paused, searching for the right words. "The comfort I found in her arms seemed hollow. I grow weary of mindless connections and am thinking of taking a wife." Seeing Sebastian grimace at the idea of forming a more lasting attachment, he changed the subject. "I am reopening the town house on Grosvenor Square. Care to join me?"

"You know I do not," Sebastian growled.

They strode from their sparring room down through a massive foyer to the prodigious Calydon library. Anthony closed the door, not willing to face Sebastian's butler nor the housekeeper's exclamations at their improper state of undress.

"Do you intend to rusticate here in the country when you

now know how imperative it is for you to find a duchess?" Anthony asked, sinking into the single armchair. He assumed a casual pose, legs splayed wide, although he felt anything but. He purposely flattened his voice, burying all trace of pain. He wanted to talk about anything except the letter their father had sent his personal solicitor, along with the family solicitor and God knew who else.

"You know how I feel about acquiring a duchess. You *will* be my heir, Anthony." Sebastian poured amber liquid into two glasses and handed one to him.

"I will not!" Anthony's voice lashed with such vehemence Sebastian paused.

"Anthony—"

"Do not challenge my decision, brother," he said, accepting the drink.

"It is your right. Not because that bitch splayed—"

"Be careful, Your Grace. The disgust you feel for our mother is understood, but you will not malign her, even if you do not claim her." He surged to his feet, prowling to the windows overlooking the estate lawns. Restless energy burned through him. "She was unhappy, and I have forgiven her for her transgressions."

"I have not, and will never forgive her. The position that she placed you and our sister in—If it becomes known, Constance will be shattered. She doted on the old man."

"And that is why we cannot challenge the claim," Anthony stated, clearing the hoarseness from his voice. "I have spoken to Mother. I did not ask for justification of her actions, though she offered it with tears aplenty. Her tears I did not want, only the truth. And it seems I am, indeed, the replica of the Viscount Radcliffe. I was blind to not see Constance's and my resemblance to her lover all these years. So damnably blind."

Sebastian came to his side, and they stood looking out upon the palatial estate of Sherring Cross. "This is yours as much as it is mine, Anthony. If not by blood, by virtue of the dedication and the wealth you have funneled into the estate to help raise it to the glory that it is today. You should be the rightful heir, to this and to my other estates. If you can never inherit it, I lay the blame directly at her feet." The bitterness in Sebastian's voice did not escape Anthony.

He sighed. "I do not. I blame the man that I once respected. The man whose admiration I worked so hard to win. I blame our father, whom Constance loved wholeheartedly and bitterly grieved when he passed. The father she thought loved her in return, but who left her exposed to scorn and ridicule if you dare to name me, my children, or Constance's children, as your heirs." He knocked back the brandy appreciating the burn that traveled to his stomach.

They were silent for several minutes before Sebastian spoke. "I know you are avoiding discussing the contents of Newport's letter."

Anthony tensed, shifted, and met his brother's intense scrutiny.

"Father sent me a copy of the letter. I know what it said," Sebastian confessed.

Anthony felt the blow sharper than Sebastian's fist. "So you know he has disowned me in every possible way?" Anthony quirked his lips. The pain that sliced through him at the admission, he had not expected to feel. It was not as if the old man had been overly fond of him growing up.

"He has not disowned you."

"You defend him?"

"I do not, but he has not disowned you, Anthony. He did not proclaim your parentage to the world."

"He has instructed the family's solicitor and mine of the circumstances of my and our sister's birth. He ordered the information be made public if you attempt to allow me to inherit any of the entail. If that happened, Constance would be faced with social ostracism of the worst kind." A circumstance he would likely kill to spare her from bearing.

Distress flashed through Sebastian's eyes. It could not have been easy on him to discover that his sister and brother had been labeled bastards, and that their mother had been unfaithful. But the fact was, Anthony had been cut off by a man he thought was his father. A man he had tried to emulate, and had excelled in his studies at Eton and Oxford in order to please.

Anthony could almost forgive the old duke for revealing his own circumstances in such a manner, but the condemnation from society that would befall his mother and Constance was unforgivable. His kind, vivacious sister, who had charmed the *haute monde* for the season, would be shredded.

The disdain that would be shown by the upper echelons when they discovered his illegitimacy had a laugh bleeding from his lips, though he was anything but amused. An impotent fury had been eating at his insides. The family would have to stick together with their full wealth and power, but still, no one would accept either sibling's hand in marriage.

"Constance's children will be branded. My children as well. And for what?" he asked, raking a hand through his hair.

"We should delay telling her as long as possible," Sebastian said.

"When have we ever lied to each other?" Anthony demanded, even though he agreed. At only seventeen years of age, she had enjoyed her first season immensely. He wanted her to hold onto her innocence a little longer.

"It may never come out." Sebastian's voice was implacable. "I will ensure it never comes out."

"She deserves to know." Despite the devastation it would cause her, he felt he owed their sister the truth. And yet, he doubted he could tell her. Much as he had, his sister had always sought an explanation for their father's coldness. He knew she deserved honesty, but he would hold onto the secret a little longer.

"Constance has much to recommend her—blue blood, wealth, her wit and intelligence, and her beauty. I have rejected a dozen offers for her already. But she needs more time. She is waiting for her prince charming to sweep her off her feet."

He and Sebastian knew every hurt, every disappointment, every hope she had in relation to their believed father.

"As we speak, she is preparing for the Grahams' ball, and, by the way, is in need of an escort."

"Our mother will be there," Anthony retorted, picking up the decanter from the side bar and refilling their glasses.

"I have no faith in our mother's capabilities as a chaperone. It was under her tutelage Constance entered the card room at Lady Brunel's ball and offered to deal for Lord Williamson," Sebastian snapped.

Anthony's laughter rang through the library. "Fine. I will go," he agreed.

Against his better judgment, his mind returned to Miss Peppiwell. He wondered idly if he even had the right to think about her. Or about the beautiful Lady Jocelyn, who even now probably expected their betrothal.

He must disabuse her of the idea immediately, of course. She deserved better than the likes of him.

He was a *bastard*.

Unlike his brother, Anthony wanted a family, children of his own. The mindless pleasures he had found in his mistresses' arms over the years had lost their luster. He wanted a deeper connection, one he was sure existed…even if Sebastian insisted it did not. Anthony's sexual tastes had always made him wary of debutantes, but he'd come to realize not even mistresses could soothe his appetites, so why not indulge himself with a wife?

He clenched his jaw. But now that was impossible.

He could not marry without informing his intended of his bastardy—it would be unforgivable to deceive a woman like that. But the moment he confessed his shame, any proper lady would flee from him and the very real possibility of society's condemnation that came with aligning herself with a bastard.

He slammed down his glass with a growl and strode from the library toward the stables, the pointed sword of his ignoble birth suspended above his head.

He did not want a mistress.

He could not take a wife.

So, what was left?

He dearly wished his erstwhile father were still alive. Never before had he so desperately wished to strangle another man with his bare hands.

Chapter Four

Phillipa sauntered into her family's parlor energized by the restful slumber from which she'd finally roused herself. She'd needed it badly, for her sleep had been dogged with nightmares these past few weeks. Not to mention the last two nights filled with dreams of a very different sort—featuring a pleasing pair of emerald-green eyes doing things to her that was far better forgotten.

This morning's long slumber had been welcomed, despite missing breakfast. The only thing to mourn was her morning ride with her Aunt Florence, the Countess of Merryweather.

"Good afternoon, Mama." She smiled at the fetching picture her beautiful mother, Katherine Augusta Peppiwell, crème de la crème of Boston society, made perched on the sofa nearest the windows with the sunbeams lighting her coiffed red hair with fire.

It was her mother's routine to view the lords and their ladies as they strolled past the Peppiwell's Mayfair town house.

Her mother poured a second cup of tea the moment she

espied Phillipa, immediately launching into her favorite topic. "You must do everything in your power to secure a marriage, my dear. Your father and I are depending on you. Payton has gone and fallen in love with the Viscount St. John's son. It may be years before he inherits the title."

Phillipa faltered, and she rolled her eyes. She had no intention of ever marrying and it seemed her mama had no intention of not pressuring her to do so. "Mrs. Pettigrew wanted to know if lamb with lemon sauce would be acceptable for tonight's dinner, Mama."

"My dear, you must stop this penchant for ignoring everything I say about you finding a suitable husband," her mother snapped, then raised the dainty china to her lips and sipped delicately—something completely unlike her.

Their foray into London society had changed them all into something Phillipa hated. She did not understand why her parents wanted to remain in London, but her mother and sisters loved it. They adored the glitter, the gossip, and the scandals that could occur over any small mishap, and bubbled with excitement over the few balls and soirees they had been invited to.

Doing exactly as her mother accused, Phillipa pulled a letter from the stack of newspapers and journals that had arrived earlier. Gladness and relief surged through her when she noted the bold scrawl of Brandon Thomas, her dearest friend. She sank into the sofa facing her mother to read.

"Are you listening to me, Phillipa?" The rattle of the china had her looking up to meet the turquoise eyes of her mother.

"Yes, Mama." She slit the seal with the letter opener and read the missive carefully. Shock stabbed through her at the news it carried.

"Are you quite well? You've gone pale," her mother said.

The letter slipped from Phillipa's hand, and she stared blankly at her.

Brandon had gotten married.

She swallowed as pain tightened her throat. She did not love him as she ought to, but to know he'd so easily abandoned his promises to her, hurt. She stuffed the letter in her pocket and forcefully pushed him from her thoughts. "Mama, you know I do not wish to marry."

"Phillipa," her mother snapped, then swung a furtive gaze toward the footman who waited at the door.

Phillipa waved her hand, dismissing him.

Her mother lowered her voice. "You know that servants gossip, and it was Lady Prescott's own butler who recommended him to us." Her teacup and saucer clattered as she placed them on the walnut table that separated their sofas. "I can only imagine what she'd think if she found out—"

Phillipa cut off the tirade before it could start. "Mama, you know I *cannot* marry."

"My dear, *must* you persist in referring to that unfortunate incident? We are all working hard to fulfill the plan my sister has drafted for you," she admonished.

That unfortunate incident. Pain squeezed Phillipa's chest, along with the shame her family kept insisting she should feel.

The door to the parlor swung open and Lady Merryweather waltzed into the room. She wore a bright purple riding habit with a matching hat. The rosy glow in her cheeks indicated she had just returned from her morning ride.

"My dear niece," she gushed, pulling off her gloves.

"Aunt Florence." Phillipa tilted her cheek for a kiss, frowning at the excitement that sparkled in her aunt's eyes. They were a perfect mirror of her mother's, and the only feature they shared as twins.

"I saw you dancing with Lord Anthony at Lord Calvert's ball. I have been bursting to question you," her aunt crowed.

Phillipa's heart thumped. She loathed the excitement in her aunt's voice, never mind that her pulse jumped with traitorous pleasure at the reminder.

"Phillipa," her mother screeched, "why have you not said anything?"

"Mama, it was just a dance."

"You were the *only* woman he danced with," her aunt stated gleefully. "He disappeared shortly afterward, leaving everyone in a fine twitter. Lady Nelson and the Marchioness of Gale accosted me this morning in Hyde Park. Lord Anthony is very wealthy, has impeccable breeding, and he is heir presumptive to Calydon. It is common knowledge his brother has vowed never to marry. Lord Anthony is a most eligible bachelor." Her aunt fairly vibrated with enthusiasm.

Phillipa would be lying if she did not admit her own interest in the man. But a stab of regret swiftly brought her back to reality. A gentleman with such impeccable bloodlines would never consider her for a match. He could only view her in one light. Her encounters with Lord Orwell had made that much glaringly clear.

"He is considered the catch of the season. Happily for us, he is still available. You could not hope to align yourself with a greater family than Calydon." Her aunt beamed.

Her mother harrumphed at her lack of response.

"You have two wonderful suitors, my dear. The family will be greatly elevated if you snare Lord Anthony, but even if you do not, Lord Orwell and Lord Hoyt are both fine catches," Lady Merryweather murmured conspiringly with a wink.

Since capturing her own English lord several years ago, Aunt Florence would only be satisfied when the Peppiwell girls were also wedded to noblemen.

"If we were in Boston, I would not be pressured to marry." Phillipa sank deeper into the sofa, wishing she could disappear in its depth.

Her mother glared at her. "If we were in Boston, we would be pariah because of the unfortunate—"

"I vow I will scream if I hear of the *incident* uttered from your lips again, Mama."

"Phillipa!"

She struggled to stay calm at the sharp admonition from her aunt.

"You must marry, child, for your sake and for your family's." Her aunt sat down next to her and clasped her hands. "No one in London knows of the incident and we must keep it that way. Your sisters will desire good matches, and therefore you must be aligned with a respectable family."

"We are no longer in America, and your father needs a proper entry into British society. Our fortune alone is not enough." Her mother sniffed in affront. "I find it so indelicate to be discussing money."

"Oh, Mama." Phillipa felt a pang of annoyance. They had been a wealthy family in Boston before a series of unwise investments by her father had seen their fortunes dwindling rapidly. He'd been convinced taking his business ventures across the sea to England would provide the opportunity he needed to recover. And it had. Since coming to London, he had found wealth in the textile industry and the soap business. More so than they'd ever had in Boston.

Now he had a notion of expanding his business into an empire. But for that he needed investors. Credible and influential investors whom others would follow. Her father's business partner, Lord Orwell, was a start, but a stingy one of late. Her father needed a more substantial connection to attract the wealthiest investors.

In Boston, Jonas Peppiwell had been respected, his influence wide and welcomed. But here in London, her father was nothing, a mere uncouth colonial merchant, not a nobleman, and therefore well below society's notice. Even the gentry thought him inadequate to mix with. It mattered not that he had amassed a fortune that rivaled the wealthiest lord…it was *new* money.

His daughter's connection to a British family of esteem would open doors for her father to build the empire he dreamed of. She hated that he believed that could only happen if he rubbed elbows with peers. But, she hated even more that in dealing with the *haute monde* it was most likely true. The family had hoped her aunt being married to the Earl of Merryweather would provide the entrée her papa needed, but so far, it had not.

Her aunt's grip on her fingers tightened. "It is more than your father's merchant status we must overcome, my dear niece. I have also had to deflect sly whispers about you. Whispers that hint you may have secrets in your closet… secrets from Boston."

She froze as she met her aunt's gaze. It could only be Orwell spreading tales, the wretched man.

"If it were not for the patronage of the Lady Gale, my dearest friend, I would be hard-pressed to quell the rumors," her aunt said with a frown. "You simply cannot become the victim of scandal again. The best solution is to marry quickly, and to a family that commands utter respect. You have been dancing with Lord Hoyt for weeks and he refers to you as his close friend. You will either need to accept his offer of marriage when it comes, or refuse his invitations to ride with him and to attend picnics."

Phillipa winced. Oh, how she despised *London* society. Any actions by her, however innocent, could excite comment and malicious speculation. She had endured that once—had devastated her family, and had friends she loved turn from her—when all she'd wanted was to be free of society's ridiculous rules.

She ignored the sympathy in her aunt's eyes and quelled the heat that burned in her veins. She desperately wanted to be alone. To think and to feel something other than the disgrace they insisted she must feel. For months all they had spoken about was the unfortunate incident. Yet, to her, it had been one grand adventure.

But now she was impure, and not fit to marry anyone of quality. Lord Orwell had told her so, boldly, and in no uncertain terms. And it was no doubt true, for it was impossible to reclaim one's virginity.

Not that Phillipa cared. She had other plans. And *she* would follow through, even if Brandon had deserted her.

"Are you not feeling well, my dear? Your cheeks have taken the most remarkable shade of red."

"I…" She straightened her spine and cleared her throat several times before responding. "Just a slight touch of headache. I think I will rest for the remainder of the day."

She gently removed her aunt's hands, gracing her with a wan smile. Lady Merryweather's lips curved in return, but worry glowed from her eyes.

"We only want your happiness, my dear," her mother burst out anxiously.

"Yes, Mama." Phillipa demurred, knowing her mother and aunt would not stop their campaign until they married her off. Not to just anyone, but to a nobleman. She grimaced. She had no desire to marry a priggish fop who believed himself more elevated than she.

The traitorous image of an audacious green-eyed lord danced mockingly through her mind, and she banished it with a huff.

"Please remember Lady Graham's ball tonight. Oh, and Lord Orwell left his card earlier. He will call this afternoon," her mother said expectantly.

Phillipa scowled, her stomach curdling in distaste as she excused herself. She loathed her father's business partner. Since being in England, she had attended several balls, soirees, and musicales. Orwell was always present, watching her like a predator. A devious, disgusting, unprincipled predator she'd been stupid enough to trust, misguided by what it meant to be a lord and a gentleman.

She would never make the mistake of trusting a *gentleman* again.

Not even ones with tempting green eyes.

Her chest squeezed as she heard the crinkle of stationery and was reminded of the letter she'd stuffed in her pocket. *All* men must be untrustworthy, she realized, thinking of its contents. She had hoped and trusted Brandon would fulfill his promise to her. Never had she expected him to send word, instead, that he had gotten married.

Oh, the fickleness of love, and the perfidy of promises.

Let this be a lesson to her.

Chapter Five

Anthony rested his elbows on the balcony railing, a cynical smile twisting his lips. He watched Lord Hoyt twirling Miss Phillipa Peppiwell with vigor around the ballroom floor. Hoyt's massive frame moved with unusual grace, and his face had a look of a man in love. His dance partner looked resplendent, sheathed in a voluminous yellow satin gown that enhanced her frame exquisitely. Her expression bore the same cool look of indifference he recalled from their meeting at Lady Calvert's ball.

Anthony forced his gaze from her and scanned the crowd, watching Constance with discreet protectiveness. She was dancing with Earl Fullerton, whose mother kept a more obvious watch on the couple. Anthony's own mother, Lady Radcliffe, was lounging idly by the refreshment table. She was a powerful matriarch in her own right, more from being the dowager duchess of Calydon than from the title she currently held as Viscountess Radcliffe.

Bitterness shuttered Anthony's gaze as his mother laughed, glowing in her social power. A power she had no notion might crumble instantly. The familiar feeling of rage tightened his gut, and he knew he needed an outlet in the warm, willing body of a woman to drive back the darkness that edged him.

His gaze swung to Lady Wilkinson, knowing her statuesque, voluptuous figure was his for the taking. His lips quirked in a jaded smile as he met her gaze across the room. The smile she returned was of pure, heated invitation, despite her husband's presence as he conversed behind her.

Distaste filled Anthony. The swell of her bosom did not entice and the sly way in which she wetted her lips left him cold. He doubted he could ever again lie with a married woman, their fickleness now abhorrent in a whole new way. Adulterous liaisons were the norm among the *haute monde*, but he found himself weary of it all.

And yet, he fleetingly wondered if he did the right thing in dismissing Georgina. He could be ensconced in her arms within the hour, driving deep into her, finding the release that would give him brief respite.

A flicker in his periphery had his gaze homing in on Miss Peppiwell. The vibrant red of her hair was unmistakable as she darted between two young ladies, making for the periphery of the immense room. He arched his brow as she peeked out from behind a large potted plant, glancing about surreptitiously. He scanned the crowd and found Lord Orwell. A salubrious smile curled the man's lips as he spied her. She scampered away, dashing out through a side door and stopped. She straightened from behind the door, pivoted, and dashed across into the billiards room.

Anthony chuckled at her antics, moving along the mezzanine balcony to keep her in his sight. The billiards room door did not lock from the inside. After kicking it in frustration, she opened it and peeked back out into the hall. From where he stood, he saw the predatory anticipation on

Orwell's face through the windows that adorned the upper half of the walls. She spotted Orwell and closed the door, none too gently.

Ah, where was the ice maiden now? This was more like it.

Anticipating her next move, Anthony considered briefly, then hastened to position himself appropriately.

Sure enough, she rushed to the outside windows, slid one up, and swung a foot over, flashing delicately shaped ankles in the process. How she managed, all corseted up and with that huge bustle, he couldn't fathom. She slithered over the sill, ran up the narrow steps—and ran smack into Anthony. He swept her through the outside doors, pulling her hastily down the terrace steps.

"My lord!"

He ignored her furious whisper and drew her toward the edge of the garden that was cloaked in shadow. He turned to her, gazing over her face with intense curiosity.

She took several rapid breaths before she drew herself up and finally spoke. "You have rescued me again, my lord."

"Ah, so this was not your way of enticing me into a clandestine affair?" he asked, his tone silky smooth.

"Certainly not." Her voice could not have sounded more bitingly cold.

He reached forward and pressed a finger against her lips to halt further speech. Her lips parted, and the moistness against his finger sparked a flare of arousal through his veins.

"He comes, be silent," he whispered low in the dark.

He watched as Orwell trotted down the stairs toward them. His gaze scanned the dark recesses of the garden, and the blinding fury that chased his features had disgust stealing deep in Anthony's gut. After a few tense seconds Orwell departed, his walk rigid with rage.

Anthony's blood ran cold. "Why does he hound you so?" he asked, though the answer seemed fairly obvious. The bigger question was what made Orwell think he could get away with it, when the lady clearly did not welcome his attentions.

"He pursues me for dances incessantly."

"You fled Lord Hoyt's embrace, ducked through the hallway, sneaked into the billiards room, and actually climbed through a window, all to avoid dancing with Lord Orwell?" he queried blandly.

Orwell's palpable rage was hardly over a slighted waltz. She was lying.

"Yes. Thank you for the assistance, my lord, even though quite unwarranted." She sounded anything but grateful as she made to leave.

He halted her, capturing her chin in his hand with firm intent.

"Lord Anthony!"

He tilted her face toward the dim lamplight, scrutinizing her shuttered expression.

"My lord, you take liberties I have *not* granted you."

Her frigid beauty illuminated in the faint light struck him. His interest in her was of a wholly carnal nature, he reminded himself. He felt no guilt at the thought, as he did not subscribe to the notion that seduction was solely a gentleman's domain. He believed in mutual pleasure, and respected that each party willingly indulged.

Yet, he hesitated, attempting to relinquish the urge to taste her lips. He had a certain obligation to Lady Jocelyn, after all.

Or did he?

Admittedly, he'd entered into that...situation...before discovering he was a bastard. Lady Jocelyn would no doubt run screaming from him when she found out. And he didn't blame her.

He resolved to write to her immediately and relieve her of any obligation to him. He'd have to word his dismissal of her carefully, but firmly. Take all the blame on himself, although he would stop short of full disclosure. No need for that.

But Phillipa… She was a different matter. She'd intrigued him the other night, to the point of considering taking her as his bride. And she did the same now. In fact, more so than ever. And honestly, Phillipa didn't strike him as the kind of woman who would care that he was born on the wrong side of the blanket. Her acid remarks about the strictures of society had hinted strongly at that.

Anthony wished to find his pleasure, with her lips beckoning him so. Unfortunately, the woman he wished to woo, to ravish, and possibly to wed, stood before him, indifferent to his charms and completely immune to his touch.

Hell.

She trembled slightly, and his gaze sharpened. Because of him? Perhaps she was not so indifferent, after all.

Or were her trembles just residual from Lord Orwell's pursuit of her? That possibility, and recalling the vicious sneer on the man's face, unsettled him. "Do you need protection from Lord Orwell?"

Shock flared in her eyes, which she quickly doused. "Protection?"

"Yes." They'd already been through this at Lady Calvert's ball. She knew the power he wielded.

She hesitated for a long moment, then said, "If I needed such assistance…at what price would it be offered?"

"There is none," Anthony assured her.

She regarded him with thinly veiled disbelief. "Your offer is generous, my lord, but unnecessary." Her lips curved in a cool smile that belied her flattering words. "Your concern for my person is deeply appreciated. You have only just met me, yet your kind, gentlemanly nature—"

Her teeth snapped together as his amused laugh cut her off. He sobered, delighted by the expressions that chased across her face. Affront, annoyance, and then chilly smoothness once more. He would banish the ice maiden yet.

"Orwell is reputed to be a sneaky bastard," he said. "I would willingly offer protection to anyone, should they become entangled with him. My offer stands indefinitely, Miss Peppiwell."

"And you insist you are making your offer as a gentleman, with nothing asked of me?" Her disdainful gaze said she expected he did it for anything but gentlemanly consideration.

"I require nothing in return, Miss Peppiwell," he assured her. He did not need to understand what drove Orwell. The man's rage when she'd slipped away from him was enough to have warnings clanging in Anthony's head. "If my own sister were involved in some folly, I'd hope someone would be kind enough to render her assistance without stipulations," he said, hoping she would unbend and confide, nonetheless.

Miss Peppiwell stared at him incredulously, in clear disbelief. He wondered what had caused such a young woman to become so cynical.

"I thank you again for your generous offer, but I require no such assistance. I bid you good evening, my lord."

She started to leave and he grasped her arm. Unable to resist the lure of her, he leaned in, dipped his head, and skimmed his lips over hers. He felt, surely, a statue had more animation. He deepened the kiss, searching for a response. She remained cold, her golden eyes strangely luminous in the dark. He lifted his head and gazed into her upturned face.

He found it uncommon that she had not reacted at all. She neither returned his kiss, nor slapped him in feminine outrage. And yet, there was that simmering heat he sensed, just below the surface of her chilly facade. A part of him was darkly curious as to how far he could push before she reacted. Before it crumbled and she threw herself into his arms.

Or perhaps he was merely fantasizing.

"I wonder what makes you tick, Miss Peppiwell," he mused.

A quicksilver of something flared in her gaze—a fraction of widening, a quiver of interest—then she went as cold as a wintery night. And he knew then, with certainty. It was all for show, a carefully contrived shield. To protect her from what?

"Not you, my lord," she retorted. "Now please remove your hands from my person." She wrenched away from him—and twisted her ankle in her haste. She cried out in pain.

"Be still." The sharp lash of his voice made her pause.

A gasp escaped her as he lifted and carried her deeper into the shadows, to the garden bench. He set her down gently and dropped to one knee, raising her foot in his hand.

"What are you doing?" she demanded in a shaky voice.

"I am determining if you sprained your ankle with your foolish impulse to flee."

"My impulse was not foolish," she snapped. "You kissed me without consent."

She made a small growl in her throat when he did not choose to respond. He found the sound utterly arousing. He lifted his eyes to hers. "Forgive me. I will not do so again without your permission."

Surprise chased her features. She frowned and then bobbed her head twice. He disliked that the wariness remained, and he ensured he was gentle as he examined her.

He probed her ankle with efficiency and she winced only once. "Does it hurt here?"

"No, the pain has already eased."

He nodded, distracted by the silky feel of her stocking-clad calf. He stroked her ankle with his fingertips, and he knew he did not imagine the hitch in her breathing. He lifted his head, curious to see what he would find. Stark desire. The bald hunger in her gaze shook him. She leaned forward and his hands clenched reflexively on her ankle. She hesitated, swallowing, and he watched the struggle, anticipation eating his gut. His mouth went dry when her tongue darted out and wetted her bottom lip.

Never had he wanted to ignore a female's wish so badly and press his lips to hers. But he would be damned if he would kiss her again without her at least making the first move. Even if it killed him.

...

The heat of Lord Anthony's hands burned through Phillipa's stockings, and she desperately wished he would release her. He was the devil himself. She'd been so tempted to tip up on her toes and lick his lips. The desire had been so visceral that she reacted without thought, and now she might have to endure a sprained ankle for the rest of the year.

On second thought, it might be a blessing in disguise, preventing her from further outings.

Moonlight spilled down the steps into the garden and his dark blond head shone under the silver beams. She had not had a chance to look at him closely tonight, unaware that he was present at the ball until he aided her flight from Lord Orwell.

Lord Anthony's black frock coat fitted his broad shoulders well—exquisitely, she decided. He wore a dark green waistcoat that perfectly matched his eyes. He was thoughtful, and devilishly handsome, and she needed to resist his advancements on all levels.

His gaze came up, catching her unguarded assessment. His lips curved with sensual intent and her heart jerked. She shivered in reaction, and it halted his slow raise from his crouch, like a predator sensing weakness.

Holding her gaze, he dipped his hands under her skirt, his grip lightly circling above her ankle. A blistering need to feel his arms around her surged through her, and her heart slammed against her rib cage. She sat rooted to the bench, disbelieving what she allowed. She had never permitted any of her suitors to touch even her bare hands after the promise she'd made herself.

She smoothed her features, drawing upon all her resolve to not betray her thoughts or feelings. "Are you quite through?" She doubted her voice had ever been colder.

His chuckle rolled over her, gifting promises of heated delights. She swallowed, wetting her lips that had gone dry. He homed in on her mouth and his hands tightened on her ankle.

"Unhand me, my lord."

"Anthony." His soft drawl was pure temptation as he slowly released her.

"I beg your pardon?"

"I trust we have gone beyond formality, Phillipa."

She almost moaned at how he said her name. As though he tasted it on his tongue, like a fine wine before swallowing.

"I must examine you thoroughly. Will you permit me to continue?" The teasing in his voice charmed her.

She nodded mutely, wondering if she was insane. She shuddered, her body throbbing under the sensual onslaught his finger evoked as they trailed up her leg to her shin, pressing and probing. Her eyes clashed with his, and she could not suppress the heat that rose in her cheeks, lighting them on fire. "I have no broken bones, my lord. You may now unhand me."

His laugh was soft and rich. "What will make you react, Phillipa?"

She knew he was testing her, but she sat rooted. Her every sense was attuned to the fingers that skimmed ever closer to the heat of her. She could not move, enthralled by the spell he wove. Need twisted through her veins and her resistance weakened.

Her blood thrummed as she felt enslaved by the spell he created even without kissing her, and by the wicked gleam in his emerald eyes.

"Tell me to kiss you." His quiet demand had her pulse spiking further.

She blinked in surprise at his hopeful look, her gaze falling to his sensual lips. "I— My lord... I— Kiss me." Shock traveled through her as the words spilled from her lips in unfettered need. Her heart begun to clamor, sending a dizzying rush of desire coursing through her veins. Before she could even think to retract her offer, he moved forward, capturing her lips. Anthony's kiss stole her resistance and the scorching heat of his mouth obliterated the last of her icy barrier as he began to devour her. Her lips parted in a soft moan of complete surrender, and his tongue slipped into the depths of her mouth.

Speech fled, and her mind churned with arousal. His fingers leisurely skimmed farther yet up her stocking-clad legs, where he hooked his finger in her garter, pulling at it teasingly. Hunger spiked to the core of her, and she trembled. She had never felt such fire from a mere touch. He slipped his fingers under her bloomers, tugging at the fine linen that protected the core of her from his touch. A deep weakness invaded her limbs. She withdrew her lips from his, panting.

His roguish mouth captured her lips again and a moan of want escaped her as pleasure swamped her. He shifted his hand and the slit of her drawers parted. She mewled against his lips, trembling as he ran his fingers through her damp curls. His tongue thrust past her lips, dancing with hers in a shockingly provocative duel. She gasped as he gently eased a finger into her. Her legs instinctively widened, accepting the lightning that slammed inside her. She purred against his lips as he teased her so deliciously.

"You feel like silk," he growled.

His voice was the catalyst she needed to save herself from his sensual spell. Horror slashed through her and she wrenched away, scrambling backward on the stone bench. She pressed her hands against her flushed cheeks, desperately hoping to cool them down. She could not believe she had allowed such intimacy. He must think her a wanton harlot!

She surged to her feet, wet and aching between her legs. Fear sank into her that she had allowed such actions. It mattered not that several times since their encounter at Lady Calvert's ball she had thought about that audacious kiss he'd stolen. She knew very well that nothing good could ever come from trusting a lord. Certainly not in this way.

He was a scoundrel, and she had fallen prey to his caresses, a touch that even now she wanted to sink back into. She inhaled shakily, resisting the need.

It was her damnable adventurous spirit that continually tempted her with wickedness. She knew firsthand the perilous consequences of indulging in such folly. So why did her traitorous body persist?

"You, sir, are a blackguard." Her voice came out shakier than she intended.

"And you have the sweetest lips I have ever tasted."

She froze as desire surged through her. She spun, hastily fleeing back to the ball.

Slipping discreetly into the mansion from one of several balcony doors, she desperately wanted to avoid Orwell, but knew she might actually be safer in the ballroom where he was. She could easily resist Orwell, but Anthony's touch aroused need.

"My dear, where have you been?" Her mother fluttered toward her, looking askance. "Lord Hoyt said you went for fresh air. He waited patiently, but now he has danced twice with Maryann Potter!"

"I went to the retiring room, Mama. All is well," she rasped, still unsettled.

Several gentlemen had claimed spots on her dance card, and she eagerly accepted the distraction. She threw herself into enjoying the ball, dancing the quadrille and the cotillion several times. And yet, she kept an unwilling watch for Lord Anthony, and this greatly angered her.

An emerald waistcoat that glittered under the light of the chandelier drew her gaze. At last he entered the ballroom, unruffled as if he had not taken great liberties with her. His slow prowl across the room toward Lady Galveston had heat pooling low in Phillipa's body. The roll of his hips and the power in his limbs had her imagination soaring.

What is wrong with me? Never before had she reacted to a man so.

She trembled as Lord Hoyt swept her into a quadrille. She danced almost mechanically, her mind swirling. What if Lord Anthony made a similar offer to Orwell's because she had not controlled her unruly desires? Dread clouded her thoughts until she feared panic would snare her.

"What do you say, my dear?"

She forced herself to meet Lord Hoyt's gaze. He had the most expectant look on his face, and his eyes glowed with happiness. She could not fathom what he had been talking about. She gave him a blank smile, to which he gave an approving grin. She must have passed muster to some concern of his.

"My dear, may I speak with your father tomorrow?" Lord Hoyt's words finally broke through her fog.

Speak with my father? Phillipa's muddled mind tried to understand what he spoke of. He looked so eager, his boyish smile making him more handsome. She assessed him as he waited for her answer. Hoyt did not rouse any feelings of lust in her. Orwell had not either, but she had once thought she could possibly be intimate with him.

This inappropriate, raging need to feel a lover's caress and the force of his hips upon her, had only been brought on by Lord Anthony's touch. She felt flushed from her head to toes. Probably her papa had been correct in his assumptions; she was indeed a harlot.

"No need to blush, my dear," Hoyt murmured solicitously. "My mother understands the *tendre* we have formed. I know it is soon, but I am sure your father will welcome my suit."

She stared at him, nonplussed. *Surely, this was a jest.* "Lord Hoyt."

His hands tightened on her waist as he swung her around with unusual grace for someone so stocky. "Please call me Vincent, my love."

She gave him a weak smile, reluctant to crush the earnestness on his face. She enjoyed his company immensely. But she did not want him to develop affections for her. She had been careful to not allow him any kisses at all, but he still was determined to move their relationship further. Rumors were whispered of his impoverished estate and she was an heiress. She had drawn swift conclusions about his interest. Yet, he seemed so genuine a person. "My lord, I do not think it wise to call on my father tomorrow."

"Any man would consider himself fortunate to win your hand, Miss Peppiwell."

"Why?" she questioned bluntly, irritated by the way he clipped her name. Anthony's soft drawl of her name was smooth and sensual. She turned her mind from such thoughts and focused on Hoyt. He seemed flummoxed, and she took pity on him. She smiled, hoping to temper the acerbity that had been in her question.

"You are kind enough to dance with young bucks that trip over their own feet. You engage in discourse with the servants when you believe no one is looking. You are patient where others would be short. I also think you make people feel beautiful."

His murmured praise had her gaping.

She forced a smile to her lips, stunned at his charitable thoughts of her. Her heart stalled at the look that flashed in his eyes. It was need. Yet she knew the minute she confided her secret to him, he would turn on her, just as Orwell had done. Hoyt was too honorable, too much of a conservative *gentleman* to consider taking an impure bride. "Please accept when I say I do think your company enjoyable. I am just not ready for marriage." She knew she chose her words poorly by the relief that shone in his pale eyes.

"Say no more, my love. I will wait a few more weeks."

She hesitated to be clearer—that she had no intention of placing herself under the restraint of a husband. She nodded, not looking forward to the day when she must be more forthright. Her aunt was correct; she needed to be more careful in how she danced and conversed with a man.

The quadrille ended and she murmured her excuses, powering through the crowd. She needed fresh air. The walls pressed in, and the need for escape chafed inside her.

Outside, the air wafted over her skin and she shivered, welcoming its cold bite.

She swallowed nervously as her eyes scanned the crowded balcony. She searched for Lord Anthony, if only to prove to herself she was not drawn to him. The minute she spied him, her heart raced and desire teased at her body. Surreptitiously, she watched him for endless minutes. To be truthful, she was charmed by the man. Not by any witty banter he'd exchanged with her, but the fact that a man of his reputation and stature danced willingly with the wallflowers and conversed with the hawkish matrons of the society. She had not expected him to mingle and laugh so freely, as if their encounter in the garden had left him totally unaffected.

She swallowed tightly as she remembered his hands skimming so hotly between her legs. He had touched her with such boldness. The memory seeped through her composure and her heart clamored that she had allowed him such intimate exploration. She desperately tried to shore up her resolve.

Oh, God, she had to speak with her closest friend, Lady Elisabeth. Phillipa had found Lady Elisabeth one of the few people she could trust, and she gave it to her unreservedly. She would pay her a visit without delay.

"Phillipa?"

She spun around to see her sister, Payton, approach, looking flushed and slightly tousled. She was so opposite to Phillipa in appearance people tended to be flummoxed when they realized they were sisters. Payton had their father's looks—dark and exotic auburn hair, dark eyes, sun-kissed skin that was freckle-free, and so many curves her corset did little to tame her figure.

Phillipa glanced behind her sister to see the Honorable Lord Jensen St. John, as he emerged from the garden's edge, trying not to look in their direction. She drew Payton to her, subtly fixing her mussed hair. Scarlet flags blazed on Payton's cheeks and Phillipa looked sternly at her. Clearly, St. John had been less than honorable in the garden.

"I know you are already halfway in love with him, Payton. He has been courting you for three months now. But be very careful of the liberties you accord him," she scolded, unable to endure the thought of Payton being callously used. She was an innocent, and wholly ignorant of the vile ways men could behave. Especially so-called gentlemen.

"Oh, Phillipa, he has asked me!" Joyous laughter spilled from her sister, warming her with its infectiousness.

She returned her exuberant hug, laughing, too. "Are you sure?"

"Yes. He will call tomorrow to speak with Papa. Hopefully now Aunt Florence and Mama will be less adamant that you marry." Payton winked conspiratorially.

Phillipa laughed again, looping her arm through her sister's as they walked into the ballroom. "Tell me all, Payton—except the part that has your lips swollen and your hair mussed."

They walked into the crowded room, and she immersed herself in her sister's happiness, grateful to leave her thoughts behind. She already feared Lord Anthony would become troublesome. She needed one night of basking in someone else's joy before accepting the doom she had so willingly heaped upon her own head.

Chapter Six

A volcano lay under Miss Peppiwell's cool surface. Anthony had seen it, experienced it, last night. The ice had cracked and what peeked from under it, he'd not expected. Her eyes had glittered with ire, and her cheeks had flushed so becomingly at the audacity of his intimate touch. But there had also been raging hunger, one that had spiked an uncontrollable need inside of him. He could imagine what she would look like in the throes of passion, his cock sinking into the tight heat of her, encouraging her to take all of him.

God, he wanted her.

He had not intended for their kiss to traverse the path it had taken, but the readiness she had responded with roused and enthralled him. Her wet heat at his intimate caresses had only drawn him more. He'd watched the expressions chase across her face in rapid flicks of emotion—anger, bemusement, desire, then embarrassment. She had been clearly mortified by her vivid response.

He found her incredibly enticing.

Despite his enchantment, he had no bloody reason to

push her so hard and so soon. Lord, the look on her face when he'd released her from their intimate embrace. Her confusion and humiliation had made him feel like a complete heel. It had been a while since he'd been so relaxed and free with a young lady. That was the only excuse he could think of for his ungentlemanly pursuit. No matter how hot or fast her body had accepted his advances, he should have been more mindful of her sensibilities.

He frowned, hands in his trouser pockets, staring out the window at the newest crumbling estate that was now his. Why was he so drawn to her? Her beauty was frigid, so unlike the women he was normally attracted to. And yet, she possessed a sensuality that shimmered beneath the chill, like a desert mirage.

But it was more than her beauty and sensuality that attracted him. He was curious about her. Such a bundle of contradictions, she was.

What had placed such icy reserve in her eyes? Why did Orwell pursue her?

A fork of lightning speared through the sky, startling the horses being led to the stables by his groom. He pulled himself from his musings. He had been too immersed in understanding the confounding Miss Peppiwell.

Dozens of gardeners, workmen, and tradesmen worked tirelessly to restore the massive Palladian manor house he stood in. He had found it several months ago during one of his visits to Lord Calvert's estate in Hampshire, and had taken steps to purchase it. Something about the lonely beauty of the place had struck a chord inside him.

The huge structure held over two hundred rooms. The mass of weeds and vines that had choked the lawns had already been cleared, but the manor itself had a long way to go.

His brother's voice interrupted his thoughts. "This is a

solid investment."

Anthony had been so deep in thought he'd not heard Sebastian enter. He glanced at him, noting the approval glowing in his brother's eyes. "Yes. I've always thought this area the best place in Hampshire to acquire property."

Sebastian strode into the breakfast room, arching a brow at the glass in Anthony's hand; then went straight to the sideboard laden with scrambled eggs, bacons, sausages, kippers, muffins, toasted bread, sweet cakes, and several pots of tea.

"How did you convince Hutchinson to sell?" he asked around a mouthful of bacon after he'd seated himself at the table.

Anthony shrugged. "He had a price, and I found it."

"It is impressive, the work that has been accomplished in a month. The only issue is your staff. Your butler is an ornery cuss," Sebastian grumbled.

"I have no idea where Mother found him. I gave her full rein in hiring for the estate."

Coolness chased his brother's features at the mention of their mother. He did not deign to acknowledge Anthony's mention of her.

"I gave Constance leave to decorate as she wished as well," Anthony added.

"I noticed the dragon motifs embroidered into the drapes. I must confess I am pleasantly surprised by its beauty."

Anthony laughed. "She insists that dragons are our coat of arms. I fear we regaled her with too much ancient dragon lore, growing up."

Sebastian nodded with a grin. Anthony took in his windswept hair and the carefree way he appeared. It was a rare day when he looked so relaxed. Sebastian needed a steady woman, a mistress, given his views on marriage. A willing female body would go far to soothe the edginess the duke displayed more days than not. However, Anthony did not broach the topic, knowing how Sebastian felt about mistresses. The scar that flayed his left cheek was reminder enough of why he categorically refused to acquire another. It must be a dilemma—eschewing both temporary and permanent liaisons. Anthony did not know how he managed.

Cobalt-blue eyes met Anthony's. "I'm returning to Norfolk. Care to join me?"

Norfolk was where the Calydon ducal estate and his brother's home, Sherring Cross, lay.

"No, I have business to take care of in town." He frowned at the reminder. "What do you know of Lord Orwell?"

Sebastian's brows rose. "Not much. His father died while he was away at Eton, so he inherited the earldom quite young. But instead of squandering his inheritance like most young bucks, Orwell managed to grow it. He takes part in several ventures that we have also invested in. Why do you ask?"

Anthony hesitated for a moment; then confessed, "He is pursuing a young lady I am interested in."

"It is not like you to squabble over a mistress. Let the lady choose," Sebastian said mildly.

Anthony snorted, swallowing his drink in a gulp. He rolled the glass between his fingers. "I am referring to a young *lady*." He glanced at Sebastian, now frozen with a mouthful of eggs, and chuckled at his stunned expression. "I fail to see why you are so shocked, Your Grace."

"I have never seen you show a marked interest in any young society miss before. You have been blathering about marrying lately, but I did not realize someone had caught your attention."

Anthony hadn't spoken to him of Lady Jocelyn. A good thing. His brother would scold him for his behavior, which bordered on unchivalrous. He must absolutely remember to send her a note tonight, before he left for London. He couldn't make himself call on her in person. He would feel too guilty over the disappointment in her eyes. He consoled himself that her distress would be strictly over losing his fortune, not Anthony himself.

He came back to the present, and Miss Peppiwell. "She is an American heiress, new to our shores these six months past."

"And Lord Orwell courts her. But you are interested in making her an offer?"

Anthony contemplated his brother's words, his eyes gazing unseeing out to where the gardeners were working furiously to clear brambles and thistles from the eastern side of the property. He studied the expanse of his estate with emotional detachment, and tried to do the same with Phillipa. He poured himself another drink and sipped his brandy before answering, carefully composing his thoughts.

"Under the circumstances, I do not plan to offer for anyone until I have given my tenuous social position more thorough consideration."

Sebastian scowled and started to comment, but Anthony cut him off.

"And no, Orwell doesn't court her. He hounds and presses himself upon her at every opportunity. I have seen her at more than one ball, and he is always there watching her. If he is not watching, then he is touching her aggressively." Anthony's voice grew terse. "You should have seen his face when she fled into the gardens, escaping his lecherous advances. His rage was almost tangible."

"So, he is not a jilted suitor?"

"I have asked the lady, but she is closemouthed. Yet, I am concerned."

Sebastian put down his fork to study him. "What are you going to do?"

"Your man of affairs, Hawke. I'd like him to put a tail on

her."

"Are you afflicted?" Sebastian snapped, his mouth parting in shock.

"I am worried about her. And it would be from a discreet distance." Anthony swirled the liquid in his glass before swallowing its entire contents. He grimaced at the burn going down.

"Very well. I'll see what I can do." Sebastian rose from his chair and strode to stand beside Anthony at the windows. They stood in comfortable silence overlooking the mysterious beauty of his land. "How long will it take for full restoration of the estate to be completed?"

Anthony glanced sideways at his brother. He knew it was not what Sebastian wished to probe, and he was grateful for his restraint. "Three months, give or take. Thankfully, I will escape the sawing and banging for the most part. I return tonight to London."

"Why not retire with me to Sherring Cross?"

Anthony made a face. "I do not want to look upon the countenance of the old man any more than I must."

"I will gladly remove the paintings."

"I find I am also curious to explore Miss Peppiwell."

Sebastian chuckled. "Miss Peppiwell, is it?" He then narrowed his eyes. "Explore? I thought you said she's a young miss?"

"She is. Nineteen or twenty, I wager."

"Then, what makes you think she will be open to your *explorations*? And is it wise, considering you don't plan to offer for her? I never thought of you as a despoiler of virgins, Anthony."

Anthony ignored the severe disapproval in his brother's admonition. Desire lanced through him instead as he remembered the hunger in her response—her moans and gasps, and the tightness that had clasped his finger. He could imagine how she would squeeze his cock.

However, he also wanted to know her beyond her bedding responses. "I assure you, I've no intention of ruining her. Merely…testing the waters."

She interested him. Considerably. What he intended to do with that interest was another matter, which he needed to carefully contemplate before acting to land himself in trouble he did not want and she did not need.

Sebastian's gaze drilled into him. "You told me Georgina broke down and cried at what she labeled the 'depraved desires' you made her feel. A young, sheltered chit would surely run screaming from your brand of exploration."

Anthony grunted. Georgina, his former mistress, was a widow and more than open to a man's advances. The first night he had taken her, she had orgasmed until she lay limp, unable to twitch. He had been somewhat shocked on his next visit at the recriminations she'd heaped on his head. The lady had claimed not to enjoy the wanton desires he so clearly made her feel. With less than a month together, he'd moved swiftly to dissolve their attachment, impervious to her tears and pleading. Apparently, she'd enjoyed him more than she wanted to admit to herself.

But Anthony wanted a woman who wasn't appalled by physical pleasure, and sought it eagerly.

Something he suspected was true of Miss Peppiwell. No, something he *knew*.

He prowled to the breakfast sideboard, heaping kippers, scrambled eggs, and bacon high on his plate. He poured more brandy into his glass.

"So, tell me more of this young lady," Sebastian invited.

Ah. So, not restraint. Merely delay.

Anthony shrugged, resigned to the interrogation. The duke was singular-minded when he chose to be. "There is really nothing to tell."

"You are heading to meet our man of affairs to *spy* on her. Even I realize the madness in the notion. Don't tell me there's nothing behind that."

"Orwell is dangerous," Anthony murmured. He was sure of it. The tingle in his gut and the prickle in his nape he'd felt at the rage in Orwell's features still haunted him.

"Why is it our problem?" Sebastian asked.

"Mine, not ours," Anthony corrected.

"Don't be an idiot," Sebastian growled, moving to pour tea into two cups. "Anything that affects you this deeply, affects me."

A laugh rumbled from Anthony as he accepted the teacup Sebastian held out to him, saying nothing when his brother firmly removed his glass of brandy.

"She interests me, that is all."

"I do not think she merely interests you. You deny you plan to make an offer, yet you are concerned enough to put a man on her. And you wish to *explore* her."

Anthony grunted. "Fine. I want her, but it is a bit more than that. And I may be contemplating courting her, but not until I am certain we suit." There. That was a reasonable excuse.

"So, you are not averse to connubial bliss with her. You are obviously attracted to the girl. Why the sudden caution? Not two weeks ago, you said you wished to—"

The studied, smooth blankness of Anthony's face froze his brother's words in midsentence.

Fury surged from Sebastian's eyes. "Do *not* tell me you will not marry because of what you found out."

His brother had always been too perceptive by half.

Anthony gave a stiff, mocking bow. "I am a bastard, Your Grace. My sons will bear that stain."

"Your sons will bear your name proudly. Everything you have will be theirs, and all my unentailed property will be deeded to them."

Anthony gulped his tea before answering, treading carefully.

"Thank you," he said evenly, "but I have enough wealth to last several sons and daughters a lifetime. And I am damn proud to know it was acquired by my own efforts and not… *his*. But the stigma of my birth that would follow my wife, my heirs, and my daughters is undeniable. How could I ask anyone to willingly endure that? What woman would want a bastard for a husband?"

It was the powerful Duke of Calydon who stared haughtily back at him. "If she loves you, she would bloody well endure, and be damn happy to take you."

The savage intensity of his brother's exhortation soothed the tension that had been building in Anthony at the topic. It was good to be so well loved and highly valued by the man he admired most in the world.

"My rank and wealth will enable us to defy society's precepts, if it ever becomes known," Sebastian assured.

Anthony wondered if his brother really believed that.

"So, you swear you have not bedded this chit?" Sebastian demanded.

"I have not. Even if I wished to… The lady is an ice maiden." He exhaled slowly. "Or…she would have you believe she is. But, indeed, I touched fire last night."

"Ah. Enough fire to have you thinking seriously about her, despite the reservations you now feel."

"I find myself intrigued by her reticence, and the hidden passion that dwells within her. She hides behind a facade of indifference, but I have glimpsed enough innate sensuality within her to hold me spellbound," Anthony confessed.

"Might it be because she is American, with a different way of expressing herself? Americans are quite a different breed than the silly chits we've both been running from for almost a decade."

He felt Sebastian's speculative glance, and met his gaze with cool aplomb, knowing what was coming. "Go ahead and ask."

His brother merely raised his brows. Anthony wondered if he had been mistaken in thinking Sebastian would have asked him how an innocent chit would handle his so-called depraved desires.

Heat sizzled in Anthony's veins as he remembered Phillipa's shivers and moans. He doubted he'd ever had any female respond to him with such abandon. She'd tried to bury it, but he had seen it in her face. Had felt it in the wetness clinging to his fingers from a fleeting caress.

He had lost three mistresses because of his passionate nature between the sheets. Apparently, no honorable female would behave the way he'd wanted them to. Though, they had opened their legs to his needs willingly enough for baubles and a roof over their heads. Despite her vehement protests, even Georgina had always writhed in ecstasy at being tied to the bed and spanked, crying for more even when he indulged in his darker sexual desires.

He shook his head in bemusement. Perhaps it was time he found a way to suppress his urgings. If his mistresses had been unable to accommodate his needs, he doubted a respectable wife would be willing to indulge them.

And yet, he thought Phillipa's sensuality would be able to match him, if anyone could. And he suspected she would be more than willing to try.

But his bastardy was another matter. Any wife of his would have to contend with the likelihood of that public humiliation.

He walked over to the windows, giving his back to Sebastian, each thinking, no doubt, of their different demons.

Anthony despised the sword edge he was balanced

on. He kept waiting for the knowledge of his parentage to roar through Society. Sebastian believed they had the social standing to withstand the repercussions. Hell, he believed they could crush it with sheer wealth and power alone. Anthony did not necessarily doubt that. His brother could be a ruthless man, formidable when crossed.

What affected Anthony most, and would savage Constance, was that the man they called father could be capable of such hatred and ugliness against them.

Anthony clenched his fists. The coward had held onto the secret, using death as a way to avoid the fallout, knowing exposing it would exact the cruelest revenge upon his wife, because of how much she loved her children. Now the evil wretch was safely in his grave — a place that Anthony dearly wished he could rip him from, so he could beat the hell out of him and send him back to it himself.

Chapter Seven

Anthony rode Thor through the crisp morning air, inhaling the fresh air into his lungs. He urged the horse faster, its muscles bunched and its gait lengthened as it thundered along the Serpentine path of Hyde Park. After his dawn meeting with Sebastian's man of affairs in one of the seedier parts of London, he welcomed the clean orderliness of the park.

The meeting had gone remarkably well. It ended with both of them clear on the nature of the tail he wanted on Miss Peppiwell, as well as to the duration. He needed to satisfy his suspicions, and would only remove the guard when the lady revealed the nature of Orwell's obsession.

The park stood nearly empty, with only a few riders braving the early morning cold. Anthony drew on Thor's reins as a flash of copper gold caught his attention. A horse cantered slowly across his path, its rider clothed in vibrant blue. Not many young ladies would be out of their beds this early. Pleasure suffused him at this chance encounter with the irresistible Miss Peppiwell.

He had barely slept after Sebastian departed for Sherring

Cross. Anthony's restless hunger for her had kept him awake long into the nights. After drafting his missive to Lady Jocelyn and handing it to his butler to deliver, he'd wasted no time traveling back to London.

The sight of Phillipa made his decision to chase off his restlessness and lack of sleep with a hard ride worthwhile.

He had been toying with the idea of calling on her, but could not make up his mind without a fuller understanding of his gnawing need, and more important, where he wanted to take it.

Hidden by the branches of an oak tree, he watched her as she cantered closer. The reins dangled loosely in her hand as she sat astride the chestnut with the innate poise of an experienced rider. She rode slowly toward him, a rare smile teasing her lips.

For a moment he imagined the smile was for him. It held something mysterious, a smile that invited a man to sink into shared delights. His fanciful notions were dashed the moment she spotted him. Her smile erased in a blink, replaced by wariness. He chuckled as he recognized the exact moment she decided to canter right past him as if he were unseen. Without giving her the opportunity, he urged his horse forward, blocking her path.

She stared at him, the memory of their last encounter swirling in her leery gaze.

She wore a deep blue jacket with a matching split skirt that allowed her to ride astride. Scandalous! Her high-collared blouse was of the finest silk and the purest white. A jaunty hat perched rakishly atop her glorious red curls. Her riding habit molded her curves and accentuated the supple way she sat her mount. A vivid image of her seated on top of him, riding him with that same slow, sensual grace strangled his breath and shafted heat through his cock.

"It is not every day one sees a young lady in Hyde Park

riding astride," he observed drily. "I must say, Miss Peppiwell, you shock me." Clearly, he wasn't.

He was pleased by her tentative smile. It still held mistrust, but at least it was a smile and not a scowl. He wondered if she saw the covert glances and disapproval in the matronly frowns thrown her way. No shade of reticence or embarrassment came from her at their studied disapproval. He admired her for it. He shifted in his seat.

"In Boston, I had the most agreeable gelding. Our home sat on over five hundred acres and when I rode him I felt so free," she ventured.

"You don't feel free in Hyde Park?" He gazed at her, curious at the longing he detected in her tone.

"In London? You jest, my lord."

He glanced around the park at the morning riders. He imagined London to be a great melting pot of poor and rich, slums and grandeur, restrictions and decadence. He supposed it did have its rules, though. Especially for young ladies.

"You are most welcome to visit my estate in Derbyshire anytime you wish," he invited. He frowned thoughtfully, a bit surprised at his impulsiveness. He had never invited a female to his estate before.

Her gaze turned icy. Had he managed to shock her at last?

His laughter spilled out as he read the censure in her whiskey eyes that seemed intent on inebriating him. The memory of their encounter curled around them, tempting him to drag her from the horse and devour her lips. That would definitely shock her.

He shifted again, his riding breeches growing ever tighter. He wondered if she noticed his particular discomfort.

"My intentions are solely honorable, Phillipa. My brother and I own one of the finest stables in England, with over a thousand acres for your riding pleasure. I invite you to ride at your whim, with a horse that befits your skill and grace."

Her eyes searched his face intently. In them, he clearly saw her desire to accept. He watched the struggle chase across her face. In the end, the coolness won.

A shame.

"I thank you for such a kind offer, my lord. I will discuss it with my family, and send a note when we are available. They will be much obliged, I'm sure."

She glanced over her shoulder at a lady who pranced toward them. He was familiar with the Earl of Merryweather's wife, but only from a distance. He waited calmly as Lady Merryweather dazzled him with a radiant smile upon her approach. He tried not to be blinded by the bright pink habit she wore that was so at odds with her gleaming copper tresses.

He noted the resemblance in the elegance of their carriage and their hair. But there it ended. Lady Merryweather greeted him with a bright smile.

"Lord Anthony, are you acquainted with my aunt, the Countess of Merryweather. Aunt Florence, may I introduce you to the Honorable Lord Anthony Thornton," Phillipa murmured.

Lady Merryweather's head bobbed. "Lord Anthony, what a pleasure to meet you."

He inclined his head to Lady Merryweather, watching the speculation grow in her eyes. He gritted his teeth. He had no doubt that she was hearing church bells in her head. He noted Phillipa's discomfort, and waited for her to fill the awkward silence.

"Lord Anthony invited me to Derbyshire to view his excellent stables," Phillipa said.

"The invitation extends to the whole family, of course, Lady Merryweather," he quickly clarified. He saw Phillipa swallow a smirk.

The radiance of Lady Merryweather's smile almost blinded him. He cursed inwardly. He wanted no idle speculation. Not until he was firm in his decision to court Phillipa. The rousing sounds of hooves clomping in his direction made him ease Thor around.

Lord Hoyt approached, looking miffed and severely buttoned up. "Lord Anthony," he greeted with false joviality. His eyes pinched as he saw Phillipa was sitting astride.

Anthony felt bemused at the slight lift of her chin. He felt instinctively as if some sort of expectation pressed in on her from Hoyt.

"Hoyt," he responded, watching their exchange with interest.

He lifted his brow as Hoyt handed a bouquet of flowers to Phillipa. Red roses. She looked at them, apparently unsure of what to do, then her gaze skated to Anthony.

He allowed his lips to quirk at her lack of enthusiasm. He felt the keen stare of Lady Merryweather as she observed the three of them.

"Thank you, Lord Hoyt." Phillipa gave him a wooden smile, then buried her nose in the flowers. "They smell divine."

"Well," Lady Merryweather burst into the ensuing silence, "Lord Hoyt is invited to break his fast with us this morn. Would you care to join us, as well, Lord Anthony?"

Phillipa's eyes flared at her aunt's invitation.

"I regret that I cannot accept," he said with a slight bow of his head. "But thank you." Relief filled Phillipa's eyes at his polite rejection. Or was it disappointment?

It was good to know he rattled her. He only prayed it was in a good way.

He tilted his hat to the small party, spun Thor, and cantered off. He wished he could, but he had other pressing issues, namely arranging to have Lord Orwell put back in his proper place.

He wanted no distractions. The attentions of the delectable Miss Peppiwell would be for him, and him alone.

Whether or not he decided to seek them.

...

The ballroom of Lady Annabel Rogers, Countess of Blade, was brilliantly lit, showcasing the stunning elegance of the room and the ladies dressed in the height of fashion. The rousing strains of a waltz filtered through the air, bringing sweet contentment to Phillipa. Lady Blade's soiree was a crushing success, and the first time Phillipa had relaxed in weeks.

"It is good to see you smiling."

Phillipa laughed, twisting to hug her friend effusively. Lady Elisabeth, the oldest of the countess's daughters, glowed in a soft pink ball gown, her gray eyes sparkling. "Is he here?" Elisabeth's voice oozed contempt.

Phillipa didn't need to ask to whom she was referring. "No, I do not see him."

Elisabeth nodded. "I ensured Mama did not invite him."

"How did you accomplish that?" she asked worriedly.

Elisabeth's giggle was infectious. "It was not hard to slip his invitation out of the masses of envelopes Mother placed on the mantel."

"Oh, you are wicked. But thank you!"

"Do not thank me yet. I ensured she invited Lord Anthony." She smiled triumphantly.

"Elisabeth!" Phillipa held her breath. "Please say you did not!"

"Oh, don't look so appalled. I have never heard you speak of any man so glowingly." Her grin quickly faded to consternation. "However, in hindsight, Mama may now think I have developed a *tendre* for him."

"Oh, Elisabeth." She griped her friend's hands and drew her across the crowded floor. She grabbed a glass of champagne from a tray, needing to steady her nerves.

"This is what I mean. You are flushed, and I can see the pulse beating at your throat at the mere *mention* of him."

"It is dread," Phillipa insisted. "Nothing more."

"No, that is what Lord Orwell inspires in you. I think Lord Anthony makes you feel something else entirely."

She flinched at the quiet assertion. "How could you do this to me?" She tried to ignore the sense of betrayal that slashed through her veins. She knew Elisabeth meant no harm, but Phillipa found her actions unaccountable.

"Please forgive me." Elisabeth's voice rang with sincerity as she tightened her grip on Phillipa's hand. "I have seen you act so coldly for the past few months and have heard the whispers of you being called the ice maiden. You radiated passion yesterday when you spoke of Lord Anthony."

"I could have sworn I cursed him," Phillipa grumbled.

"Yes, but he interests you enough to make you splutter and rail. You unfroze, Phillipa. And he is nothing like Orwell. I would be remiss in my duty as your best friend if I made you think otherwise. Lord Anthony is a gentleman, through and through. Father speaks of him well. And *all* the maters covet him as a son-in-law!"

She'd thought Elisabeth understood the fear he inspired in her. That he could so easily shatter her resistance, and use her own passion against her. Perhaps ask her to be his mistress.

The fear that she might break down and give her trust to him, only to endure heartache in the end.

After their chance encounter that morning, she could not see him again so soon. She needed time to fortify her walls. She had attended this soiree at Payton's insistence, in the expectation that few people of her acquaintance would be present. She drew her hand from Elisabeth's, ignoring the pleading look in her friend's eyes.

"I will retire for a few moments, I believe," Phillipa

murmured. She turned then froze. She blinked twice, but Anthony's tall form remained. A shot of excitement raced down her spine making her grip the glass of champagne too tightly.

Damn!

She'd thought Anthony's appearance that morning at the park had been the devil tempting her. He had featured in several dreams last night that had left her shaken and needy. She had gone for an extra-long morning ride to rid herself of the sensual visions she couldn't shake. Only to find her body all too sensitive to the feel of the muscular horse beneath her. And then to run into the man himself... Lord. It had been pure torture.

She groaned as his gaze swept the crowd and zeroed in on her.

She emptied her drink in a single swallow, and glared at him.

His gaze caressed her lips, and despite herself, she shivered. Averting her eyes, she scanned the ball, hard-pressed not to notice the many feminine gazes aimed his way. Her lips curved. They all thought they were being so sly, whispering behind their fans.

Her mother threw her the most delighted smile as he sauntered toward her with animalistic grace. Damnation. He was singling her out!

Excitement burned inside at the realization that he deliberately sought her from among all the beautiful young ladies swooning over him. She knew nothing good could come of a closer acquaintance with him, but for the moment she banished the thought and simply watched him with a soft hunger nipping at her insides.

He gazed at her with a determined intent that frightened her more than a little. She'd felt his intensity that night in the garden at Lady Graham's ball, and had been intimidated. He looked dashing in a single-breasted purple waistcoat, black tails, and well-fitting trousers. His buttoned shoes shone, and the severe style of his haircut did not detract from his raw masculine beauty.

"Are you given to stalking, Lord Anthony?" She surprised herself by inquiring. The scent of him aroused the most curious sensation inside her. He smelled of sandalwood and an elusive fragrance she could not place. The deep sensual pleasure she felt at such a mere acquaintance staggered her.

His emerald eyes traced her figure. She wore a deep golden silk gown, cut low above her bosom. Phillipa knew she looked fetching with her tresses tamed into an artful cascade, tendrils caressing her nape and forehead. However, she got the feeling he'd mentally stripped her bare, and it unnerved her.

She ignored the pleased smile from her mama, her aunt, and the wink of Payton.

"Stalking, Miss Peppiwell? I think it a grand coincidence that we frequent the same social events, don't you?"

Despite herself, a smile teased her lips at the rakish grin he threw her way. "I suppose I could accept your presence at the park this morning."

"I really happened to enjoy my early morning run through Hyde Park."

She narrowed her eyes as she met the mocking in his gaze. "And why, pray tell, are you at Lady Blade's soiree?"

"Pleasure, Miss Peppiwell. Solely for pleasure."

She told herself she would not ask.

He moved closer and said in an undertone. "Since you are so rigidly holding onto the question you are bursting to ask me, I will be a gentleman and enlighten you. I find I am intrigued by a certain redheaded ice maiden with freckles and the most delightful lips I have ever tasted."

She found it difficult to maintain her cool facade in the

face of her thundering heartbeat. She stood at a loss. She had no idea how to respond, without betraying the physical desire his words elicited. Her hands tightened even more on her glass. He gently removed it from her hands, handing it to a passing server.

"Wouldn't want it to crack," he said mildly.

A prickling sensation raced down her spine. Her eyes slashed from Anthony's, and she saw Orwell watching her from his post at the refreshment table. She stiffened. He had *not* been invited, Elisabeth had sworn. Her hands shook. His persistence was becoming terrifying.

She had allowed Lord Anthony to sweep her from his clutches at Lady Graham's ball, but she admitted she was not sure Anthony's grasp was any safer. He was a far more sensual and sneakier predator, one she should avoid at all cost. Especially so, considering that she feared that she might be his willing prey. He provoked the most alarming desire with a mere caress or the gentle brush of his lips across hers. The invitation to sensual indulgence she saw in his eyes shook her to her core.

"Would you care to take a twirl in the garden?"

Her gaze whipped from Lord Orwell to meet the dark invitation that shone in his expression. He had the most beautiful, expressive eyes—dark and rich, holding secrets like the forest. "I cannot. Not without inviting unwelcome speculation."

"I thought speculation incapable of affecting you."

She arched her brow sharply. "Why would you think that, my lord?"

"You rode astride."

She did not miss the dip in his voice. "You have formed conclusions about me from the way I ride?" she asked, nonplussed.

"Was I wrong? I thought you were not one to bend to

conventions." His voice lowered further still. "Had dared to hope the freedom you seek to indulge in...lay in more than riding without a sidesaddle."

Her breath strangled. Perhaps she was mistaken, but the wild beat of her heart told her she wasn't. His eyes had stripped her to the skin, and she couldn't understand how, from a fleeting encounter, he could have gleaned something so profound about her. It was as if he sensed her weakness, like a wolf saw a lamb.

A glitter shone in his eyes, and she fought the leaden heat surging through her limbs, recognizing it as desire.

He wanted her. Possibly enough to pursue her. But to what end? Suddenly, she was petrified. "My lord, I—"

"Anthony." His gaze never once wavered from her face.

She swallowed, and persisted. "Really, I—"

"Come now, Phillipa," he chided, "I want to hear my name on your lips. Are we not friends? Intimates, even?"

She stared at him mutinously, but the teasing that danced in his eyes pulled a reluctant smile from her lips. It wasn't as if she could deny the shocking extent of his knowledge of her person.

And the miraculous thing was, he didn't condemn her for it. Didn't consider it an open invitation to disrespect her, as did Orwell. Lord Anthony seemed to...enjoy...her adventurous nature.

"Very well. Anthony."

His obvious pleasure at her capitulation warmed her, and she was afraid her protective shields were lowering much too rapidly. Not that they'd stopped him before...

"Now, if we are unable to twirl the garden, what other pleasures may we partake in?" he mused.

"If we are to be *friends*, my...Anthony, there must never be a repeat of what occurred in the garden the other night." She hated to speak of her indiscretion but she must be firm.

His brows lifted and a rueful smile edged his lips. "Forthright little thing, aren't you?"

"I assume honesty is frowned upon amongst your other acquaintances?" She slid him a sidelong glance from under her lashes. She did not wish to be coy, but she thought if she gazed at him openly, her desire for him would be far too evident.

"On the contrary. Honesty is welcomed." He held out his arm. "A dance, then?"

She did not trust his slow sensual perusal of her. Not knowing how to deal with him, she could only nod. She followed mutely, her heart thumping as he escorted her into the ballroom, her dance card dangling from her glove.

Why had he singled me out? Not tonight, for that was fairly clear. But the very first time, at the Calverts' ball, where she'd kept herself so carefully cold and closed off, doing her best to stay aloof and unapproachable. She burned to ask, but truthfully, she feared his answer. She had already blundered erroneously with Orwell, and it was a miracle that she was not already bleeding from the vicious claws of Society. Another slip, and she would be finished for certain. And she couldn't do that to her family. To her father, and her sister, who both needed her to succeed.

Anthony swept her into a waltz, the strong grip of his arms easing her into the beautiful dance. She twirled gracefully, the arousing strains of the violins igniting delight in her. The smile that burst from her lips could not be contained as she hummed to the captivating music.

"You like to dance?"

"I love dancing and music. It is one of those rare times when I feel alive."

He focused on her face and she lowered her gaze, fighting the urge to converse freely.

"Please do not."

"I beg your pardon?"

"You seek to hide behind that high wall you have erected around yourself. Please, for tonight, if only for this dance, I beg that there be honest discourse between us."

Her hand tightened on his reflexively. It unnerved her that he knew she had erected a barrier. Lord Hoyt had surprised her with his assessment of her at Lady Graham's ball, but Anthony's keen perception terrified her. She had only encountered him a few times. He should not be able to see into her so deeply.

Of course…his fingers had already been deep inside her. She shouldn't really be surprised his understanding could follow.

She hesitated, loath to expose any more of herself. However, if she could trust Elisabeth's judgment—and she felt she could—he was an honorable man. Her friend had warned her Orwell was untrustworthy even before he had so blatantly revealed his nature to her.

So, she risked lowering her shields a bit further. "My greatest passion is for music. I agree music gives soul to the universe, wings to the mind, flight to the imagination, charm and gaiety to life…and to everything else, I wager."

His approving nod had her relaxing in his arms. "Thank you."

She returned his smile. She tried to warn herself not to sink into the sensual invitation that radiated from him. He was a fantastic dancer, lissome, but with a raw, untamed power.

"So, the sincerest way to your heart lies in dancing and music? How is it your legions of suitors have not discovered this?"

Was he interested in the way to my heart? She studied him carefully and only saw teasing and objective interest. She relaxed further still, banishing the warning bells that clanged in her head. And her heart. "None of them understand my spirit."

He tilted his head. "Your spirit? Pray, tell me."

"Sometimes London is so…stuffy. Stiflingly so." She chortled. "Just once I would love to dance something scandalous and exciting and play a bawdy tune on the pianoforte."

Anthony barked out a laugh. "Good God, gel."

Lord, he was so different from Lord Hoyt's staid and quiet composure that she wondered if Anthony were real. Some months ago, she had regaled a small gathering at Hoyt's house with a rowdier version of Czerny, for which she had received the severest of tongue-lashings from her aunt. She'd been shocked to see that she had embarrassed and mortified Lord Hoyt's mother. She was actually surprised she was still welcomed in their home.

"The waltz is not scandalous enough for you?" Anthony queried.

Phillipa gave an inelegant snort. "The waltz, Anthony, is certainly *not* scandalous. It may have been considered indecent a few years ago, threatening the morality of innocent women, if you can believe that. But it is now as banal as the two-step. I fear I may have been born in the wrong time. I either belong to the past…or to the future."

"The past?" Anthony asked, seeming enthralled. "Elaborate."

"Like the primitives I've seen pictures of. Even in Boston I could immerse myself more in dancing and music than in England. It is as if the joy of the rhythm that pulses in the body has been crippled here. There is no adventure. Dances should be exciting and creative," she said firmly.

"You don't find the country-dances creative?" he asked.

"Are they? I've never been to a country-dance in England. I have attended a few London soirees, and the only things danced are the cotillion, polka, and frequently the waltz. It is as if all the exuberance has been choked under puritanical rules. One day, I hope to experience a dance that is wickedly indecent and adventurous. Failing that, I shall have to dream of being transported to the primitive past in my imagination. Or perhaps the future will be less strictly laced."

She held her breath in an agony of anticipation for his response. She felt as if Anthony's reaction to her treatise was the single most important thing she had ever waited for. Never had she wanted so desperately to trust a lord.

And prayed this one was not like all the rest.

Chapter Eight

Phillipa's golden eyes glittered, alight with excitement, intoxicating Anthony in the most curious of ways. Nothing else could account for the light-headedness he felt.

He shook his head to clear it of his fanciful notions. She waited for his reaction, and at his lack of response, vulnerability seeped into the depth of her eyes as she lowered them in embarrassment.

He tipped her chin back up with a finger. "Your passion for music is inspiring. I would love to dance the mazurka in private with you," he drawled. "And anything else you desire. The more exciting the better."

She gave him a radiant smile, and he accepted then and there he would court her. He would delve beneath her reserves, strip her layers, and whatever she wished for, he would offer to her gladly.

"I'm afraid I have always been scandalous, Anthony. I've ridden in several buggies without a chaperon." She nodded as if he'd said something. "Shocking, I know."

He liked that she teased him. "Very."

"Oh, dear. I've mortified your noble sensibilities."

They chuckled together, and more than a few frowns of disapproval were thrown their way. Anthony liked her so much like this. The icy wall of reserve had thawed to reveal a woman of warmth and passion. Need slammed into him instantly, and he cursed his weakness for her.

"I assume this explains your banishment to our rigid soils."

Shadows chased her face, only to vanish as quickly.

His curiosity deepened. "Ah, I see I'm right. Tell me, what scandal did you leave behind in Boston, my sweet?"

Her eyes widened, and he watched in fascination as she tried to erect her wall of coldness. He decided to topple it before she succeeded.

"I am twenty-eight," he declared. "And I, too, must lack noble sensibilities since I don't subscribe to the stilted nature of British society, either. I've had three mistresses, and several lovers of whom I have not, and will not, speak, as I hold the utmost respect for all women."

Phillipa spluttered at this bold confession, staring at him aghast. "I—"

He grinned back at her. "*Hmm*. I didn't think you capable of being shocked. Didn't you say you like living on the edge?"

Her eyes narrowed. Then a rueful smile curved her lips. "You are incorrigible, my lord."

"I decided I must inform you of my own licentiousness before you would tell me about whatever happened in Boston to darken your eyes so. Now that you know all my secrets, I am waiting to hear yours."

Her laughter tinkled, and she shook her head, dismissing him. "I believe I have no secrets from you, Anthony."

He was intrigued more by the naked need he saw on her face than anything else. No, her body kept no secrets from him. But it was her soft laugh that truly stirred him—fresh, crisp, and utterly captivating.

He wanted to give her everything she desired, and more. The compulsion burned deeply and powerfully.

He would have her. And soon.

...

Phillipa had to admit that Anthony was an amazing dancer, his movements embodying raw masculine power and beauty. He swung her, and she swiveled, and the heat of his hands on her lower back, burned through her gown. Just being held in his arms was sinfully delicious.

The next waltz started, and she was thrilled when he did not relinquish her. *He was dancing with me twice?*

She felt the eyes of assembled guests upon them, and for this moment in time, she cared not one jot what they thought.

She tried to ignore his questioning that hinted she might have a truly disgraceful past, but he was having none of it. So she relented, and gave him a half-truth.

"I distressed my family by attending women's rights conventions and meetings. I think they feared my wild ways would have led to my disastrous downfall. My aunt recommended dancing to soothe my excessive passion—or so she told my father."

"You chose to focus your passion on dancing. Pity."

She probed his features to ascertain his meaning. "I adore dancing, and I find it to be the only thrilling thing offered to women by society. The restrictions heaped on young ladies are frightful," she declared.

Her curiosity about him drummed at her, but she reined in the questions that buzzed insistently in her head. He had several secret lovers of whom he didn't speak, so their scandalous actions in the garden were safe from the gossips?

"Restrictions do not exist in Boston?"

"I daresay they do." Rueful laughter spilt from her lips. "However, the pretense is more subdued. I could have wed a banker or a lawyer back home, and I would have brought my family esteem. Here, my aunt is appalled at the mere notion. There, I could attend a picnic without the need for a chaperone. Here, to visit my dear friend Lady Elisabeth, my aunt insists I travel with a ladies' maid and a footman at all times. The most ridiculous thing is, it is not for my protection, but because it is appalling for a young lady to be seen walking alone. Well, a virtuous female, at any rate." She could not prevent the incredulity that rang in her tone.

He pursed his lips. "And this is what you seek to be free from?"

"False propriety, yes. It all seems incredibly pretentious, don't you agree?" Phillipa smiled at the surprise that etched his features. "I had already felt suffocated in Boston, and now in London, I am truly fit for Bedlam. It is a daunting task to understand what is acceptable by the *haute monde* and what isn't."

Her inquisitiveness drummed even louder. He had not reacted to her sweeping statements like Hoyt and Elisabeth. Perhaps there was hope for a kindred soul, after all.

"Worse, there is nothing here to dazzle the senses," Phillipa ventured cautiously, watching Anthony's expression.

"I am sure there must be other pleasures that rouse your interest." He returned the intensity of her gaze.

"I find London society exceedingly dull," she assured him.

He seemed to deeply consider her. "And what is it that will lift this banality for you?"

There was no hesitation in her response. "Freedom."

A frown creased his forehead. "Are you not free? Where are your shackles?"

"The shackles of society are invisible, but they are there, as surely as irons."

She gasped as he spun her into a dizzying twirl. A primitive thrill surged through her at how he controlled the rhythm of their movements. She flowed with him, surrendering her body to his, trusting that he would keep her safe.

The sudden realization that she trusted him rattled her. But Elisabeth was right. He thawed her frozen soul.

"Tell me of this freedom you desire," he coaxed.

The need to share swelled inside her. She tamped down on it ruthlessly, her gaze roving over his face, trying to garner his intentions. Her heart thudded. She saw only genuine curiosity.

Trepidation rushed through her. What if he was interested in her as a suitor?

Both dread and elation filled her at the thought.

"I yearn for more than what society offers. There are times I feel I am being suffocated. My aunt had a conniption because I insist on riding astride. My youngest sister, Phoebe, cannot dine with us adults, even if we are alone. What balderdash! I want to sail the oceans, ride a camel, explore the ruins of Venice, and eat French pastries for breakfast!" She gave him a conspiratorial smile, and she leaned in closer. "Have I shocked you yet, my lord?"

"I profess the French pastries were a near thing," he drawled.

She giggled.

"You cannot shock me, Phillipa. I have, indeed, already endured this very conversation with Constance."

She gave him a quizzical look.

"My sister. My brother, Sebastian, and I had to make a place for her in the dining room. She was only six at the time. She categorically refused to eat alone."

"I like her already. And this was allowed?"

"Our fath—" She felt a sudden tension roil through his frame. "Our father refused. But Constance has a way of opening her big eyes and filling them with tears that would soften the heart of the most hard-hearted jade. And Sebastian championed her. So, yes, it was allowed."

"From your tone, I assume you did not champion her?" Phillipa questioned tartly.

"Of course I did."

She studied him. There was something behind that carefully bland expression. "But if you were the one who championed her, it did not matter?" she ventured.

His shutters slammed into place so suddenly she felt startled. They whirled in silence for a few seconds. She felt unsure how far to push. He had been so warm and teasing, and she, of all people, understood the need for protective walls.

"Tell me more of your desire for freedom," he said.

His closed expression challenged her to understand him. She knew she should tread carefully, lest she reveal too much. But she'd never felt such enjoyment from a simple conversation. Or, perhaps not so simple.

"I yearn for an adventure," she confessed. "There are days I think I will go mad from boredom." She met his gaze, showing him a little more of herself, hoping he would show something of himself in return. "And I have no desire to marry, to be confined by the strictures of a husband."

She waited, holding her breath. But he did little more than smile, and say, "Ah."

"You are not shocked by that?"

"You will need more than a yearning for adventure to titillate my dissolute tastes. Even though, I am truly appalled that you might consider eating French pastries for breakfast, Phillipa. It should at least be a British confectionary."

Laughter pulsed from her. "I said the same thing to Lord Hoyt in the presence of my aunt and his sister. His sister, the Lady Henrietta, sank into the most perfected swoon I have ever witnessed, and my aunt berated me for upsetting her so. She said I must have overwrought nerves brought on by the noonday sun. I didn't bother to point out we were experiencing the dreariest of weather."

Anthony pulled Phillipa closer, enough so that her thighs brushed against his. She knew he was holding her much closer than was considered proper, and a small thrill vibrated through her.

"I thought you would love to have a little adventure right under their noses," he murmured in her ear.

She laughed, but a wave of heat shimmered between their bodies. It kissed over her skin, igniting a thrum of need within her. With stunning dexterity, he waltzed her through the French doors onto the terrace, and maneuvered her into the enclosed gardens.

"Anthony."

"No one noticed in this crush. I assure you," he said.

She came to an abrupt halt, withdrawing her hands from his. "Why have you brought me out here?" She was proud that her voice held none of the turbulence and uncertainty she felt.

"I thought to take you on an adventure."

"What kind?"

"The kind that must be experienced."

She looked into his eyes. They gleamed much too wickedly, and she instinctively took a step backward, toward the lighted ballroom. "My need for adventure must be tempered with good sense, as my aunt continuously pontificates," she retorted.

He took a step backward, into a dark alcove. He lifted a hand to her. "Come."

The strains of the music lingered in the air, its sensual notes tempting her to take his hand again. He beguiled her. She worried he could see it, and she agonized over what to do.

"And if I refuse?"

"I will discreetly escort you back inside."

God help her, but she believed him. Without allowing herself to think, she grasped his hand, and the smile that curved his lips heated her inside. He slid his arm around her waist, drawing her closer yet. The open strains of the waltz drifted into the garden.

He drew her deeper into the shadows. A gate stood open to a secret, hidden, tall-hedged garden, and her heart slammed painfully as he led her in and closed the gate. Its hinges creaked and she jumped, betraying her nervousness.

She looked around with a false calm at the stone benches and the walls adorned with vines. They ran riot and covered a long stretch of wooden trellises. A fountain stood in the middle of the inner garden. The darkness cocooned them, and the moonlight barely glinted off his golden locks.

She took a deep breath, her nerves tingling.

He shrugged out of his jacket and splayed it on a cold stone bench. "Sit."

For some reason she could hardly fathom, she did as he asked. The satin skirt of her gown crinkled in the quiet night.

Slowly, he untied his cravat.

Uncertainty made her surge to her feet. "What are you doing?"

"Sit down, Phillipa."

Her heart thundered, and she sat back down, half terrified, half thrilled.

"Are you ready for an adventure that will make you forget the banality of life, if only for a few fleeting moments?" he drawled.

The humor in his tone relaxed her, and she knew instinctively that if she said no, he would stop whatever he had in mind.

"Yes."

She did not resist when he circled her wrists and tied them together with his silken cravat. The way he studied her, it seemed as if he was testing her reaction. She shivered as he arranged her so she reclined on the stone bench, placing her bound hands above her head, tying them to the vines that hung from the walls. A disconcerting surge of excitement whipped through her at the wicked heat gleaming in his gaze.

He sat on the other end of the bench, and she desperately wanted to see his face. She could feel the heat of his regard, as it seared through her. Yet, she trusted him.

She bit her lips hard until they stung. She'd trusted Orwell, as well, and look where that had gotten her. They were both lords, belonging to the same set of social values and perceptions.

"What adventure is there to be found with me tied to a trellis?" She could not disguise the tremor in her voice. What was she doing?

Anthony leaned over her, his body almost blanketing hers. His eyes glittered with something she could not identify. "I will not take your maidenhead. I swear to you," he whispered against her lips, then claimed them in a brief but alarmingly pleasurable kiss.

She froze. Her muscles locked. *My maidenhead?*

"Isn't this what you wanted? Adventure?" He gave her a lazy, roguish smile. He kissed her again, sharp and brief.

Oh, God. Was this what she wanted? Adventure, yes. To be free, yes. But could she trust his word?

She believed with all her heart he was nothing like Orwell, or even Lord Hoyt. But what if she was wrong?

"If you are uncomfortable, I will release you," Anthony said, "and I will ensure you arrive back inside without being seen."

His promise and lack of pressure reassured her as nothing else could. She prayed she wouldn't regret her impulsiveness…

but she wanted to experience this with him. Whatever he had planned for her.

Her voice was husky when she spoke. "Take me on your adventure, Anthony."

He held her gaze for a long moment, searching her face. When it appeared he found what he probed for, a smile touched his lips, and he eased back into the darkness. She waited in an agony of anticipation and need for his touch. It came on her ankles. She groaned, melting with desire. The soft, satiny feel of her gown slid sensually against her skin accompanied by the crackle of petticoats as he pushed them to her waist.

His rough chuckle rolled over her. "It seems you have already started on your adventure. No bloomers, Miss Peppiwell?"

She laughed shakily. "Not wearing any is my way of thumbing my nose at the haughty ladies of Society."

The quirk of his lips was pure, heated sensuality. She gazed at him, enthralled by her own nakedness. And by the way he looked at her. The cool night air kissed her skin, but it did little to calm the fire that burned inside her. She was painfully aroused and gripped by emotions she had never felt before. Her skin was fevered. She pulsed with wetness, though he had not touched her intimately as yet.

He parted her legs, and she felt suddenly vulnerable as she lay before him, completely exposed. Her heart thundered, and she shivered as the breeze cooled her burning skin.

She admitted she wanted him. There was an ache, deep and unrelenting, inside her that she wanted to be filled and banished, and only by him. Yet, a knot of doubt held her from releasing the passion that bumped so insistently at her resistance.

Confusion marred her brows. What was he doing? He anchored her splayed thighs to his shoulders and dipped his head, kissing her deeply in the sensitive place between her legs. Her back bowed and an unfettered shriek ripped from her lips. A pleased rumble escaped him at the sound of her choked gasp.

Shock and arousal vied for equal attention. Her hips moved rhythmically as his lips ignited her most intimate nerve endings, the pleasure sharp and searing. She tugged at the silken restraints but her actions merely tightened the cravat. She was desperate to do something, to hold the head that was tormenting her so erotically between her legs.

His mouth pressed deeper between her thighs, doing the most sinfully delicious act, one she could never have imagined. Fire scalded her body as she met his eyes over the length of her body. His tongue rimmed her entrance, and she whimpered. The green of his eyes glittered, and he intensified the erotic kiss, stabbing his tongue deep within her.

Her mind hazed from the undiluted heat his tongue generated. The desire he roused felt dark and needy, and it scared her. She had never felt anything like the inferno that raged through her whole body under his skillful ministrations. Yet she felt as if this was only the beginning.

The sensuality that stamped his face as he rose above her had her arching her hips in needy welcome. "You are so wonderfully responsive, Phillipa." He crooned against her lips before claiming them.

She moaned, tasting herself on his lips. Her hips rolled in hunger, and she desperately wanted to be filled. She'd felt pleasure before, but had never encountered anything quite like this—this was fire.

She frantically tugged at the restraints, wanting to grip his head and feast on his mouth. She growled in frustration as they wouldn't yield. Shivers racked her frame, and she became painfully aware of the hands that rested so casually against her quivering stomach.

He pulled his lips slowly from her.

A fiery blush heated her face. "You are diabolical, my lord."

The seriousness of his gaze forced her to focus. "If you do not desire marriage, then what do you need?" His voice was rough with arousal.

She hesitated. "To do what I wish, where I want, when I want, without condemnation." She could not disguise the raw ache in her voice for more, for him. "Please," she urged.

He snaked his hands down and cupped her mons possessively. "What do you wish to do?"

Excitement thundered through her. "I will not be your mistress. I will never be anyone's mistress," she said.

"What will you be to me, then?"

"Your lover," she rushed out, shocked at her own declaration. "I do not desire marriage, nor wealth, nor your protection. But, I want you, Anthony. I want to explore what is between us without fear or recriminations."

"And when your husband discovers your lack of maidenhead?"

She willed her body to relax under the tension that gripped her. Words begged to tumble from her lips, but instead she said, "I will never marry. I could not bear to be so confined." She let the honest desire bleed from her gaze, lowering her barriers so he could see truth.

A frown chased his features but quickly disappeared.

Her breathing stilled when his fingers combed through her saturated curls to find the core of her pleasure. His thumb flicked against her nub and pressed. Her hips surged, and her body wept for him.

He took her lips and drank in her cries, his finger teasing the rim of her entrance without delving in, his thumb circling her knot of pleasure. Her hips strained against his hands, and she mewled into his mouth in edgy desire, desperate to feel fulfillment.

His kiss deepened as he worked two fingers into her swollen core. She yelped against his lips, tugging at the silken bonds, twisting as pain pinched her, mingling deep with the pleasure.

"I am not an easy lover. I want to sink my cock into the tightness of your body until you beg me to stop because of the burn. But I won't stop, and then you will be begging for me to take you hard, as the pleasure ignites within you." He twisted his fingers, working them inside her deeper, his thumb still circling her knot of pleasure.

Waves of delight swamped her senses and when she exploded in ecstasy, she did so soundlessly, stunned by the way he brought her to the pinnacle of ecstasy.

After long moments of endless pleasure, she floated back, and he deftly untied his cravat. He pulled down her dress and eased her into a sitting position. Sensuality was etched in his features, but there was an aloofness there that unsettled her.

Without giving much thought to her actions, she rose from the bench and pressed her lips against his. He stilled, and then his arms slowly banded around her, deepening the press of their lips. Her soft sigh was swallowed by his lips. She needed it, the gentleness after the storm he had just carried her body through. His tongue twined with hers in deep, languorous strokes. Her shivers subsided and lethargy invaded her limbs. His retreat was slow, as if he was unwilling to release her.

"I do not share," he said against her lips.

She smiled, her heart surging with a sort of gladness. "Neither do I," she responded, tipping to nip at his ear. "I want adventures. I want to tour the teeming life that is London. I want to visit the famed Decadence gaming hall and watch the women dance the cancan."

"I do not think it is adventure you seek."

She arched a brow, admiring the way the moonlight threw

his patrician features into sharp masculine beauty.

"You desire complete ruination, Miss Peppiwell."

"Is this disapproval I hear from the man who just lifted my skirts and kissed me between my thighs on a stone bench at Lady Blade's soiree?"

"Never," he assured her. "I heartily approve of your wicked behavior, my sweet."

She loved how easily he laughed. "How will we meet? My aunt chaperones me almost all the time. She may be searching for me, even now."

"You won't be missed in this crush."

He spun her around, and she held still as he artfully rearranged her hair. He did so with an expertise that flummoxed her. "It is unusual for a gentleman to know how to coif a lady's tresses." She wondered if he'd done these sorts of things with his mistresses.

He grunted. "I have a sister."

She twisted around, trying to make out his features in the moonlight. "You arranged your sister's hair?"

"Constance has an inquiring spirit. She was the youngest, and as secluded as we were at Sherring Cross, it fell to me and my brother to entertain her, which included a lot of designing her hair to befit a princess."

He nudged Phillipa to indicate he was finished, and she turned to him, captivated. "So you played tea parties?"

He gave a lazy smile. "We did everything with Constance. We dressed her hair, played with dollies, and had tea parties with the Queen and her ladies in waiting. Believe me, it was a blessing when it evolved into swimming and fencing."

"She sounds very accomplished." Phillipa inhaled, then plowed ahead. "Anthony, why do you want me?"

Even though she had decided on this affair with him, she still doubted his motives. She wondered if she would take back her offer to be his lover in the cold light of morning without the sensual strain of music in the air, and his tempting presence luring her to unknown pleasures.

He shuttered his gaze quickly enough, but she saw her question had startled him.

"For my part, because of my views on marriage I've wanted to take a discreet lover," she explained, "which I know you'll be. You're breathtakingly handsome and interesting and irreverent, and I wanted you from the moment I saw you at Lady Calvert's ball. I want to throw propriety in the wind and simply enjoy my life." She tilted her head and regarded him. "But why are you interested in me?"

"You are available," he drawled blandly.

She jerked back, stung. Pain sliced through her at his callous answer. "I—" She hated that he'd said it that way, as if she were a common doxy. She did her best not to show her profound hurt. "I see."

The familiar feeling of shame tried to rise up, but she refused to indulge it. Ice crept over her, chilling the warm satiety in her flesh to cold indifference. She straightened her spine and started to walk away. "I bid you good evening, my lord."

"Most young ladies would have slapped me for my temerity," he said.

She halted, anger flushing her cheeks. "You were testing my reactions?" she demanded.

At his silence, she spun and walked with rapid steps out of the garden.

"Phillipa."

"Go to hell," she said, and kept walking.

In an instant he had grasped her arm, spinning her to face him.

"I'll tell you why. You captivate me. I admire your thirst for adventure…your joy for freedom, your vivacity. I want you because you rouse me as no other woman has done in years, if ever. And I want to burn in the passion I see beneath your cool gaze, a passion I suspect will satiate my every need. I want to see you bound to my bed with silken ropes as I spank you, fulfilling your every dark fantasy. Then I want to ride you hard and deep, until neither of us can move for spending."

She gasped at his vivid descriptions…and at the chaotic cravings that erupted in her body at the forbidden pictures they created in her mind.

He saw her expression, and gratification swept over his. "I want total control over your body and your pleasures, Phillipa. I believe you want the same. You will match me perfectly, fantasy for fantasy. I had thought to court you. But if you are not interested in marriage, I will gladly take you as my lover."

Heat slashed her cheeks, her whole body. *How does he see me so deeply?*

She nodded jerkily, stunned by his profound insight to a part of her she had never dared reveal to a living soul. And grateful, at least, that he understood why she had no desire to marry. "I thank you for your honesty, Anthony," she managed.

She did not linger. She couldn't. She needed to think. To work through the intense emotions that had erupted within her at his bold declaration. She fled through the gate, nimbly walking toward the side window.

Missing the shadow that lurked behind a hedge, watching her as she hastily made her way back inside.

Chapter Nine

The white silence of winter pressed in on Anthony. Snow fell in a steady dribble, dotting the land with its frosted beauty. The fireplace crackled, and his mind inevitably turned to the delectable Miss Peppiwell. She consumed his thoughts. Her vigor when she danced, the coldness she could exude, and the honest need she burned with when he took her in his arms. The sweetest lips he'd ever tasted. And the forbidden things they had explored together…

But it was her desire to be free of society that tantalized him. He had wished for the same, years ago in the face of constant disapproval from the old duke, the occasional thrashings, and the feelings of inadequacy.

She had no wish to marry. But he would entice her with sensual fantasies and tantalizing adventures, and when he had secured her affections, he would offer for her hand. How could she refuse?

He wondered what had happened to her to inspire such an aversion to marriage. Most young ladies plotted their wedding day from the cradle. He knew Constance had already decided before she left the schoolroom the month and day she would wed.

Mamas and young chits throughout Society constantly sought to entrap him or his brother. It was just his luck that the first woman to evoke such intense passion and his first real interest in marriage only wanted to have an affair. But he was determined to woo the lady, and would do everything in his power to ensure her answer would be yes.

A soft knock sounded and his ornery butler entered, his eyes blazing with irritation. "A Sir Hawke is here to see you, my lord." Interesting having a butler who felt exasperated when his door was knocked upon.

"I will see him in the library," Anthony indicated, swiping up the copy of George Elliot's *Middlemarch* he'd been reading.

A few minutes later Hawke strode into the library looking more harried than usual. He was short and stocky, with dark, beady eyes furtively scanning the room to pause on the decanters of brandy on the drinks tray. Anthony had never seen the man so distressed. Hawke hastily handed his top hat and coat to the retreating butler, then scurried over to the great chair and sank in its depth, his eyes darting everywhere but at Anthony.

"What is it, man?" he asked as he rose. He walked around his oak desk to pour the man a brandy, and pushed it into Hawke's hand. Taking a seat on the edge of the desk, Anthony folded his arms across his chest and waited for Hawke to speak.

"The gel you had me watching was taken."

"What?" Anthony demanded, instantly on his feet.

"Miss Peppiwell was taken on her walk from Kensington Gardens."

"Damn it, man!" He bent to grab the lapels of Hawke's tweed jacket. "Taken by whom? Why did you not prevent it?"

he bellowed.

"You paid me to watch at a discreet distance, not to interfere."

He jerked the man out of the chair. The brandy went flying. "Tell me what happened."

"I believe she was kidnapped. Some gent grabbed her from behind and threw her into a carriage. He then leaped in after her and the driver sprung the team into motion. I couldn't have reacted in time to stop it."

Anthony's gut tightened. "And you did not set anyone to follow?"

"I did my best, milord, on me own. You didn't pay for—"

He grabbed Hawke's neckcloth and strangled his words. The man's eyes bulged and Anthony went cold, immune to the fear that widened them. "If she is harmed because of your inefficiency, I will hunt you down and gut you," he swore savagely.

He let the promise sink in, and only after Hawke nodded, he released him. "Which direction did they travel? And tell me the type of carriage."

"It was a black lacquered. The crest was covered with a black cloth and the driver's hat was pulled low over his face. But their horses were Andalusian, some of the finest I have ever seen. They headed toward Brighton, but…"

"Spit it out man," Anthony snarled at his hesitation.

"I followed as far as Corydon, then I lost them."

Anthony's mind worked swiftly to reason out his options. "Go," he grunted. "Hire as many men as need be. Send to the west, east, and south. Discretion is paramount, but do everything you can to find her. If she is located, bring her here. Pay anyone you must to keep silent."

He opened a desk drawer, withdrawing a hefty bag. It jangled as he threw it at Hawke. Anthony ignored the man's sharp inhalation as he opened it.

"This is gold, milord!"

"Get out," Anthony ordered, fury riding him hard.

Hawke moved swiftly to obey, and Anthony strode to the gun case and grabbed several weapons. He carefully loaded his pistol and slipped it in his pocket, then withdrew his special cane, twisted its head, and checked that the hidden sabre was still razor sharp. He shrugged on his jacket, and then yanked on the bell pull.

"Yes, milord?" The butler had appeared instantly, his irritation smothered by the anger that saturated Anthony's voice.

"See that my brother gets this tonight." He scrawled a note and stamped his seal handing it to him. "There must be no delay. Find him wherever he is and deliver the note personally. He is most likely at Sherring Cross."

The butler executed a smart bow and sped from the library, a man on a mission. Perhaps his mother had not been so remiss in hiring him, after all.

Anthony stormed out to the stables, his mind roiling with the possibilities. It could only be Orwell. The knowledge settled uneasily in Anthony's gut. He would investigate, leaving no stone unturned, but the obsession he had seen on Orwell's face had been about more than Phillipa let on. He'd had little doubt before, and now it was confirmed.

Rage burned at Anthony, some of it directed at her for dismissing the danger Orwell presented. Most of it was directed at himself for not demanding a full explanation. If he had not been concerned and hired Hawke to watch her, no one would even know she had been taken. Not until it was too late.

Anthony would tan her backside when he found her. For real, not in bed play. He refused to give in to the ugly thought that he might never find her.

"Milord?" His groom scampered out of his way in alarm.

"I was not told to prepare a horse, milord."

"I'm telling you now."

With grim efficiency they saddled Odin, his fastest thoroughbred, and he launched onto its back and thundered through the gates of his estate, determined to catch the reprobate who'd thought to harm Phillipa.

Orwell may have kidnapped Phillipa to marry her by force. Or he may have taken her simply to have his pleasure with her. But either way, the blackguard would take her body against her will. Anthony's gut tightened. He despised men who raped or hurt the fairer sex. He would crush Orwell if he so much as touched Phillipa's hair.

Anthony rode low in the saddle, Odin's hoof beating like thunder as his long powerful strides ate up the distance. Orwell was ahead by at least an hour, but he traveled in a carriage. Even though it was pulled by a team of four, Anthony's single mount would be much faster.

Storm clouds darkened the sky, and the cold rolled over him in chilly waves. Despite Orwell's head start, if Anthony was headed in the right direction, he should catch up before the rain started. He sped into the windy night, hoping that Sebastian got his message informing him of his decision to marry.

Anthony would insist he and Phillipa marry if he could not extricate them from the situation without scandal. And there was a slim chance of that. Orwell would surely have seen to it that word got out of her ruin.

Before taking that step, Anthony would have to reveal the truth of his birth to her…much sooner than he'd planned. He prayed the fact he was a bastard would not turn her against him. Or worse, somehow become public knowledge. He didn't know what he would do if she refused to marry him.

But first he must rescue her from Orwell's clutches.

He sent a fervent prayer to God that he would find her

alive…and unharmed.

...

Phillipa squirmed and twisted, bucking wildly against the fiend who held her, striking him ineffectually with her parasol. She saw his fist crashing down toward her face, and could do nothing but lurch backward to avoid its full impact. The blow glanced off the side of her head. Terror exploded inside her at the look of savage enjoyment on his face at her pain and terror. The carriage jostled, throwing her against the swabs with jarring force and she dropped the parasol.

"You are a madman, Lord Orwell!" she hissed, sounding far braver than she felt. "You will not get away with this. My father will see you hanged!"

Orwell barked out a laugh. "You honestly think anyone will believe your merchant father over a noble lord? It is you who are mad, my dear girl. And I am sure your family would be beside themselves with joy *if* I decide to make you my wife."

Phillipa ground her teeth, wincing at the pain in her jaw. Unfortunately, he was probably right. Especially given the untenable position in which she found herself. Her only choice was between Orwell and complete ruination for her and her entire family.

He had come out of nowhere, grabbing her right off the streets. Regret flared that she had dismissed her maid, taking pleasure in walking the short distance to her home without someone watching her every move.

"You will ignore me no longer. I have begged, cajoled, sent you gifts, and you still rebuffed my attentions at every turn."

"Attentions? You tried to make me your whore," she spat out, swiping up her parasol again. The delicate fabric was torn.

"I asked you to be my wife…before I found out your true nature," he said, his eyes glowing with lust. "You will never get a better offer than to be my mistress. Phillipa, I desire you in a way I have never desired another woman. I must have you. You *will* say yes."

She shrieked as he came at her. She swung her parasol, smacking him in the eye. He howled, and ripped it from her hands, tossing it to the floor and reached for her again. She swung her fist at him. Pain splintered through her hand. She reeled as he slapped her hard, her vision wheeling.

"I will not be used by you!" she cried, even as despair swamped over her. No one had seen him take her, and when her abduction was discovered, her reputation would be shredded beyond repair.

It would not matter that she was the innocent victim of his despicable deed. The stain would be on her and her family. A harsh sob ripped from her chest, and fury filled her at society's hypocrisy.

The carriage lumbered along a street, jarring and jostling her as it ran over cobbled stone. She lunged desperately for the carriage door and hollered at the top of her lungs, praying someone would hear her over the din.

"Quiet!" He rapped his knuckles against her head sharply, and she cried out in pain.

Orwell was insane. She was at the mercy of a raving lunatic. Never had she dreamed he would do something so horrible and underhanded.

"I cannot wait to taste you." He moved in and wet kisses peppered her face and neck, sweaty hands tore at her sleeves.

"No!" Her scream split the air as he flung her on the cushion and shrugged off his coat.

"I must have you. *Now*."

She lunged for the small brazier by her legs, grabbed the iron handle of the grate, and swung it at him. He roared, ducking to avoid her blow, but it struck his head with a sharp rap. His savage howl filled her with satisfaction. He leaped at her, enraged, his strength overwhelming. He was powerfully built, and she had never been more aware of her own body's fragility.

"Do not do this," she cried as his hand thrust under her dress, fighting to tear off her bloomers. Her mind frantically searched for a way to deter him. "Lord Anthony will kill you if you besmirch me!"

He went suddenly still. "What did you say?" he growled, his fingers squeezing her jaw.

"Lord Anthony made an offer for me yesterday. I accepted. He will kill you for what you are doing, I promise." Fear squeezed her insides at the manic look that stole over his face. But at least he had stopped his assault.

"Have you let him touch you?" Spittle flew from his mouth. "*Have you*?" he screamed squeezing her jaw even tighter.

"I—"

He searched her face and his anger slowly turned to cold fury. Then a howl of madness ripped from him. "I saw you in the garden with him at last night's ball. If you have given yourself to him, it is I who will kill *him*." Orwell's mouth crushed down on hers, his teeth savaging her lips.

Her desperation grew as she tasted the coppery tang of her own blood. "Stop!"

"If you have given him what rightfully belongs to me, I will destroy him! The only reason your other lover still breathes is because he lives on another continent." Orwell's voice was gravelly with anger and arousal.

Fear cramped her stomach.

With a rip, he tore the bodice of her muslin gown in two and grabbed her breast through her corset.

"No!" she screamed in pain at his savage grip.

With the brute force of his muscular thighs, he opened

her legs.

A gag rose in her throat. She could feel the press of his manhood through his trousers digging into her stomach. Desperately, she searched for something, anything, she could use as a weapon. Hope surged through her as she spied the pistol that hung loosely from his jacket pocket. She grabbed it.

He was so intent on his attack, he reacted too late to stop her.

She cocked the hammer. The soft *snick* echoed through the carriage. His hazel eyes narrowed in rage.

She pressed the muzzle into his soft belly, uncaring that he might feel the trembling of her hands. So much the better. She could accidentally shoot him.

Or not so accidentally.

"Get away from me," she ordered between her teeth.

The carriage lurched, but her grip remained tight. He slowly backed away and sank back onto the cushioned seat opposite her. She thought he would feel fear at having a pistol trained on him. Instead, a smile teased his lips. The smile frightened her more than his assault.

"I will shoot you," she warned lethally. "Stop this carriage at once."

"I will not."

She raised the pistol a fraction. "Do it *now*."

"You will not shoot me. You *will* be hanged. Your family made pariahs. Not even fleeing across the ocean would save them this time."

She forced her hands to steady as she aimed the gun at his black heart.

"Go ahead." He taunted her with cruel laughter. "I am a lord. You are an American nobody, offended that I spurned her advances."

"You will not live to tell a tale," she said coldly, wishing she could end his miserable life. She desperately wanted to pull the trigger, but fear cramped her stomach. What if he was right? She would hang, her family disgraced, even though he attempted to rape her. And if they married, it would no longer be rape. It would be his right.

She had confided his obsessive pursuit of her to no one save Elisabeth, and Elisabeth's father would never allow her to testify in court. Not even to save Phillipa's life. Their association would ruin her friend, as well.

"If you move, I *will* shoot you," Phillipa vowed. "I would rather hang than let you defile me."

"One can't defile a harlot," Orwell sniped savagely.

"You will stop this carriage and let me leave. If you don't, I will kill you."

His dismissive laughter froze her insides. She gripped the heavy pistol, ignoring the growing burn in her muscles, and the jostle of the carriage as it sped her to complete ruination.

He rapped the trap door to the driver's seat to give instructions, and her heart sped with relief. Until he yelled up, "Faster! Drive faster!" His laughter echoed sinisterly.

Tears stung her eyes as she heard the crack of the whip. The carriage careened, sped up even more, and her breathing became ragged. The oiliness of his smile, the depravity in how he licked his lips had her stomach cramping harder. The heaviness of the pistol grew harder to manage. She did not know how much longer she could hold on.

She did not dwell overlong on her decision. He gave her no choice. She raised the pistol and fired.

The *bang* exploded in the close confines of the carriage. Her ears rang; her head pounded. She heard the muted neighs of the horses, the driver's frantic commands, and the carriage rocked wildly as it slowed. She acted with desperate alacrity, wrenching the door open. Before the team had fully halted and before the driver could stop her, she jumped.

And ran like her life depended on it.

Chapter Ten

"Grab her!" Orwell's cry of wounded rage spurred her faster.

Phillipa clutched the pistol to her breast, holding her torn bodice closed against the chill, and raced across the flatlands. She could see a manor house in the distance, but her breath labored in the daunting cold. She was grateful for the moon that peeked from the clouds providing her with light. She gripped her skirt, hating how the petticoats hampered her movements. She raised it high above her knees and sprinted as fast as she could. Fat drops of rain slapped her cheeks as she ran and ran. She refused to look back. The thundering in her ears grew louder, and she belatedly realized it was hoofbeats.

Oh, Lord. Her breath caught and tears splashed her cheeks. He was riding her down.

"Phillipa! Stop!" His hated voice was muffled by the wind and the ringing in her ears.

"Leave me alone!" she cried, her tears flowing with the rain.

She could not run any faster, so she turned into the woods. With brambles ripping at her hair and her lungs burning, she stumbled to a stop and spun, jerkily raising the pistol.

Her heart thundered, and she blinked, dazed, at the massive black stallion that loomed over her.

Sweet relief crashed through her as she stared into the grim face of the man she most wanted to see in the world. Her heart soared.

"Anthony!"

"Oh, thank God!" He jumped from his horse and swept her into a tight embrace. "Is he dead?"

"No!" she gasped, her body racked by a rash of shivers.

"I heard a pistol shot."

Her teeth chattered. "I fired into the cushions, to create a distraction while I fled."

The cold rain came down in torrents. She raised her violently trembling hands to Anthony's cheeks. "Is it really you?"

"You're freezing." He shrugged out of his greatcoat. "Here," he muttered, bundling her into the voluminous cloak. It was warm and smelled like Anthony, and she sank into its comfort. He'd come for her. She was safe.

Pounding footsteps came through the trees, and she gripped the pistol tight. She really would shoot Orwell this time, before she let him hurt Anthony.

But it was the coachman. He broke through the thick brambles of the forest and screeched to a startled halt when he saw Anthony. "I— I—"

His stammer was cut short in a wheeze when Anthony delivered a short, brutal jab to his throat. He fell with a crash into the thicket, choking, then stumbled off, running in the direction of the last village they'd passed.

"Stay here," Anthony ordered her.

Not a chance. The dark pressed in on Phillipa, and she scrambled to keep up with Anthony as he strode back to the carriage. His fine white shirt was plastered to his broad shoulders and rain ran in rivulets down his golden hair. He looked like an avenging angel.

Orwell drew up sharply when he saw them, quickly masking his astonishment.

"Lord Anthony," he said with a sneer, stepping down from the carriage into the rain.

Her mouth went dry at the dangerous glitter in Orwell's expression.

She started to warn Anthony, but she realized it was unnecessary. She flinched from the cold rage that gleamed from his emerald eyes.

"Are you really willing to go to the gallows over this tease? This lascivious slut?" Orwell smirked, strolling with insolent confidence toward Anthony.

Hadn't they just had this same conversation? But this was worse. They were talking about Anthony now.

Anthony did not deign to answer. Instead, he backhanded Orwell when he came within striking distance, shocking her with the viciousness of the action. Orwell snarled and charged him. Anthony grabbed Orwell's lapel and yanked him forward, then slammed a fist into his face.

Phillipa stood rooted to the spot, trembling, as Anthony punched Orwell again. Anthony gave him no quarter, no chance to retaliate. Anthony slammed his fist in Orwell's gut, doubling him over. Orwell groaned.

Thankfully, it was over almost before it started. With Anthony landing another vicious blow to his face, Orwell crumpled to the ground. Anthony casually walked toward the carriage. She stared at him in ill-concealed shock, feeling faint. Rain pasted his hair to his scalp and ran in rivulets down the sharp blades of his cheeks into his soaking jacket.

"Get in," he growled with barely leashed fury, flinging open the carriage door.

She jerked into motion, stepping gingerly over Orwell and scrambling into the equipage just as the sky opened with fury. Anthony leaped in after her and sank into the darkened shadows of the carriage, silent and cold. They sat mutely, listening to the sound of thunder and clouds pouring out torrential rain. She trembled, freezing and nervous, feeling the palatable tension in the air.

"Anthony—"

"Quiet." His voice cracked like a whip.

She shuddered. Tumultuous emotions glazed his eyes, as if he fought for restraint. She did not know how to respond to this unknown side of him. Before, he had been so sensually teasing. She would never have thought him capable of brutality. The beating he had given Orwell could have been far worse, had he truly lost control, but it made her realize how little she knew of Anthony.

She had never imagined any of this would go this far. With Orwell or with Anthony. She swallowed, tears burning her eyes, shivers racking her.

And yet, Anthony had rescued her. He had come for her.

Weak moans came from outside; Orwell had regained consciousness. She didn't dare ask what would happen next.

"Let's go," Anthony said, saving her the trouble, and stepping down from the carriage.

She scrambled after him, avoiding the curled-up form of Orwell on the ground. The cold rain caressed her cheeks like a dark omen. It shook her to the core.

And knew her life was forever changed because of this night.

They halted at the massive black stallion. "What will we do?" she beseeched Anthony, hating the rage he thrummed with. She wanted her sweet lover back again.

He drew her to him. His head slashed down and his lips captured hers in a hard, rough kiss. Her lips parted, but before she could sink into his kiss, he lifted his head again.

"We are about fifteen minutes' hard ride from my manor

house in Baybrook. We can rest there for the evening." He raked a hand through his wet hair. He looked as if he'd been about to say more, but stopped.

A crack of thunder made her jump.

"We must get there before the deluge returns," he said, looking up at the black clouds.

He leaped into the saddle and held out his hand to her. She did not hesitate to grip it, and was swung up behind him. They raced into the night as the sky opened a little more. She wrapped her arms tight around his waist and pressed her face into the hard muscle of his back. She couldn't stop her tears from falling, mixing with the drops of rain that splattered so insistently.

She had almost been raped.

She wanted to curl into Anthony, to feel his arms around her, to banish the horror and the edge of fear that still lingered. The profundity of her gratitude staggered her. Her mouth whispered words of thanks, even though he could not hear them.

The night was icy cold as they rode, stealing her breath and chattering her teeth. The sky darkened, eclipsing the stars. A premonition of her future?

The sky opened as they raced by houses they could have sought shelter from, but she understood why he did not stop. A harsh sob ripped from her. Even now he had thoughts to protect her reputation. She did not know if it could be salvaged, but she hoped so. If not for her own sake, for Payton's. She prayed Orwell would not trumpet the fact he had tried to kidnap and rape her. Instinctively, she knew Anthony would protect her.

A manor house loomed in the distant with a light flickering high from a lone window. Relief surged when Anthony turned the stallion toward it. Within minutes, they rode into the yard and he swept off the horse, pulling her with him. He handed the reins to a stable boy who ran out to meet them, and stalked toward the entry. The front door was flung open, and he marched in, issuing commands. Servants scurried to obey, and a matronly woman bustled toward them clucking her lips.

"Ach, to be out in this weather, milord."

"Prepare warm milk and food. Send it up to my room. A decanter of brandy, as well."

The housekeeper did not falter at his growled command as she handed him a towel and threw a blanket over Phillipa's trembling body.

"Thank you," she said, though it did not ward off the chill.

Anthony strode through the foyer, and she hurried after him. He made a sharp right into an open doorway. A gas lamp glowed in the room, illuminating a sizeable library. She felt numb as he sat behind a desk and scrawled a note with furious haste, then stamped his seal.

"See that this is delivered to Lady Radcliffe tonight," he ordered, and she spun to see a butler she had not realized followed them in.

"Very good, milord." The man cleared his throat. "My lord, about that other letter you bid me deliver…"

Anthony looked blank for a moment, then frowned. "Yes? What about it?"

"You asked me to give it to"—he glanced at Phillipa then back to Anthony—"the person in question myself."

"Yes, yes, and did you?"

"No, my lord. The…family has been away visiting relatives, and I—"

Anthony slashed a hand in the air dismissively. "Just see it's done. Meanwhile, get moving with the note to Lady Radcliffe. That is far more urgent."

"Very good, my lord." The butler's gaze scanned over Phillipa with curiosity before he took the missive, bowed, and exited the library.

Phillipa knew the Viscountess Lady Radcliffe was Anthony's mother, but why had he sent a note to her? He was in such a temper she didn't dare ask. Nor about the other mysterious letter—though it hadn't seemed overly important to him.

"Come with me," he said, and Phillipa's heart beat faster as her trepidation returned and her situation closed in on her. She should not stay overnight at his house. The consequences would be untenable.

Questions and dread swirled in her mind as she followed him down the hallway. Thunder rumbled, and lightning speared through the rooms they walked, mocking her. She struggled to keep up with his rapid strides up the elegant staircase. He led her down a long hall, finally stopping in front of a large oak panel door. He wrenched it open, making it crash against the wall.

"Why are you so angry?" she asked.

He darted a disbelieving look at her, tugged off his dripping jacket, and snapped, "Undress."

She stepped back warily.

His jaw clenched. "You are wet and shaking. You need to get warm and dry. I do not want you catching influenza."

Lightning lit up the room again, and the thunder rattled the windowpane. She looked to where he pointed, and saw it was a bath chamber. It did look awfully inviting. And she was, in truth, shivering with cold.

A maid bustled in and lit a gas flame under a copper water tank. The chamber held a large tub with two spigots pouring into it, one with heated water from the tank and the other for cold. In the tub, she sprinkled salts with the most delicious scent of jasmine and honeysuckle, and soon hot water was filling it.

She relented, and another maid helped Phillipa remove her wet garments. "I will see they are washed and ironed, milady," she said as she finished unlacing her corset.

Phillipa did not have the energy to correct her use of a title. She wearily sank into the soothing heat of the fragrant bath, easing the tension in her body. She yearned to sink into its comforting embrace and stay there forever.

Her stomach rumbled, reminding her she'd not eaten since her afternoon tea with Elisabeth. Hunger and uncertainty had Phillipa hurrying her bath. She dried off and pulled on a gown the maid had left for her. It was simple and of an old fashion, but clean and dry. A wobbly chuckle escaped her lips at the size of the voluminous garment. It swallowed her slender frame and trailed around her on the floor. With a sigh, she gripped the skirts to keep from tripping, and went into the bedchamber.

She froze. "Anthony."

He was still dressed, only his coat and boots had been removed. *Was he not cold?*

The fire from the hearth blazed, providing much-needed warmth. When he didn't respond, she flicked her gaze around her.

The bedroom was stunningly elegant, with masculine decor. A large canopied bed graced the center of the space, and in the far left corner stood a rather impressive oak armoire. Thick, jade-green curtains were drawn back with golden cords. The drapes and the Oriental carpets were bold colors of green, red, and silver. The blandest colors were the soft peach curtains that surrounded the canopied bed.

Clearly not a guest chamber.

Her cheeks burned. Now she understood the furtive glances the maids had given her. She *really* should not stay in this house.

She met his gaze as she stepped deeper into the room, faltering when his voice snapped at her, sharp as a whip.

"What is it between you and Orwell?"

Her heart slammed against her ribs as she caught a towel he threw at her. "I—"

"Dry your hair," he ordered roughly. "Orwell?"

"Nothing. There is nothing between us." She clutched the lapels of the dressing gown tighter, ignoring her hair.

His eyes silted and the anger flared anew. "Phillipa—"

"I can see you are angry, though I do not understand why. I want to thank you for saving me from—" She stumbled backward as he surged to his feet and in two strides stood before her.

"You do not know why I am angry?" His voice was dangerously low, and he was frightening her.

Her eyes skidded to the bed and then back to his. "No."

He raked his fingers through his hair. "Surely, you must comprehend the situation you placed yourself in," he said more calmly.

"*Me?*" She gaped at him and her own anger flared. "I was abducted and attacked! How is that *my* fault?"

"I do not blame you, Phillipa, for Orwell's atrocious conduct. However, all this could have been prevented if only you had confided in me when I asked," he said with visible frustration. "What do you think he planned to do to you?"

She trembled at the memory of her fear and revulsion. The pain of Orwell's fondling pummeled into her anew and a tear slipped down her cheek.

"So help me *God*, if you cry I will tan your backside," Anthony whispered.

Her eyes widened.

"He would have *raped* you. Beaten you bloody when you resisted. Broken you in unimaginable ways. And no one would ever have known, because Orwell would have likely ended your life afterward," he said, his teeth grinding. He was clearly more than upset. "I gave you every opportunity to seek my aid, but you chose to withhold the truth. So now we must deal with the consequences together. We will marry, whether or not you wish it."

She recoiled. "Marry?"

He gave her an incredulous glare. "What did you think would happen? I would rescue you, and everything would simply go back to the way they were yesterday? It will be a miracle if this debacle has escaped society's notice!"

"Please say no more about Orwell!" she cried, and stuffed a fist in her mouth to contain her sobs.

"We will wait out the storm. I will obtain a special license, and my mother will arrive in the morning. I asked her to send a note to your family so they won't worry."

"Thank you; I am eased considerably knowing they won't be anxious over me, but I will *not* marry," she insisted.

His eyes gleamed dangerously. "I do not think you fully understand the situation." The lethal softness of his voice slapped her more than his snarls.

"I understand perfectly," she declared, fighting to stay calm. "A cad tried to kidnap and defile me, and instead of society condemning him, judgment will be levied on *me*, and I will be forced to marry, just so society does not cut me from its ranks."

They glared at each other in a bristling silence.

"I should leave," she said.

"You shall do no such thing," he stated firmly. "The weather is fierce, and enough damage has been done for one day."

Her eyes swam. "You are being cruel."

"Phillipa…"

"Do not." She jerked from the hands that reached for her, her tears running unchecked. "I have never been so afraid in all my life. I am eternally grateful that you rescued me. I do not want to fight with you. I do not want you railing at me. I do not want to consider the consequences of my naïveté. Oh, Anthony, I only want to be held in your arms, with your touch wiping away his."

Chapter Eleven

Even with her face florid from tears, the sight of Phillipa, and her heartfelt plea, aroused Anthony more than any other woman. He felt shocked she would dismiss marriage to him, under the circumstances. No woman had ever looked at him with such naked physical need, and yet it seemed she did not share the same hunger for more.

Her rejection roiled within him like bad ale.

She could not know the anxiety that had gripped him when he thought he wouldn't reach her in time. Or the terror when he saw her in the woods, thinking he was too late. Her dress had been torn, her face stained with tears, her lips swollen and bruised. The raw relief in her golden gaze at seeing his face had been worth the relentless pace he'd punished himself and his horse to travel.

Her misery over her plight punched deep inside him. Desire flared, but he tempered it, needing to offer her comfort with his touch. He began to remove his wet clothes. He did not stop to analyze the need that seethed within him—the urge to bind her to him, to experience the fire she vibrated with. He wanted to explore every curve, taste her skin, and immerse himself in her shuddering cries.

The dart of her tongue to moisten her lips sharpened the edgy arousal he felt. He shrugged out of his waistcoat and unbuttoned his shirt with impatience.

The overlarge gown slipped, revealing perfection to his eyes. She let it slide from her shoulders and it anchored at her elbows. The sleek, graceful line of her neck and the pertness of her breasts lured him. He pulled her to him until the tips of her breasts grazed his chest. He savored the feel of her almost-naked body so intimately close to him, loving her sharp inhalation at his touch.

Desire flowed through her eyes, along with an emotion that made him halt. She shivered and swallowed, and he realized she was afraid.

She leaned into him, resting her forehead against his shoulder. The rain drummed on the roof, the wood in the fireplace crackled, and embers sparked. And still she did not move.

He grasped her chin and lifted her face. "What is wrong?"

She regarded him wordlessly, her eyes fearful. She squeaked as he swung her up in his arms and strode to the bed. He tumbled her down then captured her slender wrists and held them above her head. "Tell me. What is it?" he demanded.

Her eyes smoldered and darkened with desire, but chilling reserve crept into them trying to dampen it.

"Do not shy away from me, Phillipa." He kissed the corner of her lips.

"I have secrets," she murmured. "Ones that may repel you from me."

"You speak of the impossible, my sweet," he assured her.

She tugged, and he released her wrists. She touched him as if unable to stop herself. Light caresses danced over his neck, his face, his lips, and his shoulders.

"I am not innocent," she said softly. Her voice was a hoarse rasp, and she trembled in his embrace.

Something primitive tightened in his gut. The ice maiden was no innocent. He suddenly understood her aloofness, the iciness with which she looked at him, even now in her nakedness.

She expected judgment. Condemnation.

He felt neither. Instead, lust coiled around his insides, dark and inviting, and he welcomed it. He dipped his head, holding her gaze. He slanted his lips over hers, nipping her whenever her eyes fluttered. He wanted them open, so she could see the honest craving for her that lived deep within him. He was gentle, lips roving with soft teasing flicks instead of the hunger that gnawed at him.

He pulled away, leaving a hair's breadth between their mouths. "Neither am I."

The sweetest smile curved her lips. A groan whispered from him as he pictured them stretched around his cock. The tension slowly eased from her taut frame. She slid her arms around his shoulders, and with a contented sigh, opened to him.

He groaned as he delved deeper with his tongue to twine sensually with hers. Her hand gripped his hair, her fingers combed through it as she clung to him.

And he wondered who was the one being seduced.

Desire punched him, hard and potent. He reluctantly released her mouth. "If you want me to stop, say so now."

"No. I don't want you to stop." She exhaled shakily.

He went straight for her breasts. His mouth covered a nipple that was ripe like a berry. He rolled it between his teeth before sucking. Her hips undulated, and her hot whimpers raked at his control. He nudged her legs wide and settled between them. Then gave equal attention to her other nipple.

Her cries became more frantic, her hands kneaded his shoulder, and nails dug into his skin. He released her nipple and trailed his fingers down her throat. He shifted and trailed them farther down, resting on her stomach. She quivered beneath him with restless hunger. He skimmed even lower, and her hands tightened painfully in his hair. He combed through her curls and delved into her with two fingers. "I knew you'd be this wet for me," he murmured against her lips.

He thrust slow and deep, preparing her. Her eyes widened when he opened his fingers inside her, stretching her. Her folds were swollen and slick, and she felt impossibly tight. He trailed his fingers down the crack of her buttocks.

Her tongue darted to her lips hesitantly. "Anthony?"

He reined in the desire that twisted at his gut. He needed to slow down and introduce her to his darker passions gradually. He would take her in every way imaginable, but tonight he would start by riding her into boneless pleasure.

He stroked and caressed her until she was as needy as he was. Her hips squirmed on the bed, demanding his possession. He grabbed a cushion, easing it under her hips, then rose above her.

"Look at me," he commanded.

He drew her up so her buttocks rested on his thighs. He parted her with his fingers, lodged the head of his cock against her entrance, and sank inside an inch. She felt incredibly tight, too snug for someone who professed experience. She rewarded him with a pulse of silken wetness and a provocative mewl. He sank a little deeper, and she stiffened.

"Relax," he soothed. Her tightness had him gritting his teeth savagely.

The pale creaminess of her stomach quivered as she met his gaze. Her body resisted despite her slickness, so he ruthlessly stamped down the need to take her in one swift move. She claimed she was not innocent, but he guessed she had no knowledge of what innocent truly meant.

She thought the loss of a virginal barrier meant anything. As her lover he would devastate her sensibilities, and he would not hold back. He wanted to explore all his desires with her for he knew he wanted her as his wife.

He would not allow his bastardy to taint her or their children. He would crush anyone who threatened to allow it to surface.

He groaned as he sank another inch into her. He had never before felt the incredible sensation that arched up his spine and bowed his back. Hell, he was not even a quarter way into her, and he was perilously close to spending. His hips jerked and he sank deeper than he intended.

"Anthony!" Her nails bit into his arms and her hips recoiled into the bed.

"It will be quick." He forged forward inexorably, needing to be surrounded by her heat.

Her cry echoed in the chamber, and he froze instantly. Sweat rolled down his forehead. He slowly glided out of her, his breath hissing between his teeth. His desire heightened as he saw how her juices glistened on his thick length.

He dropped his forehead against hers, trying to cool his raging hunger. He was not a small man, and he'd always been rough in his desires. But he wanted to give her more than pleasure. He wanted her to know that she would always be comforted, protected, treasured.

That she would always be safe in his arms.

...

Phillipa had never felt such yearning from mere kisses. Yet, she felt instinctively that Anthony restrained himself. The vitality he exuded seemed leashed, and even now she could feel the tension radiating from his muscles.

His girth made it hard for her to relax. The bite of pain with the pleasure when he entered her fully had enthralled her. She rolled her hips, undulating to a need she did not fully understand.

"Anthony," she said breathlessly. "I don't want to be a lover you have to hold back with."

He froze and looked down at her.

So, she had been right. Her heart stuttered. She was swamped in carnal pleasure and he had been holding back?

Her nipples hardened even more at the look that darkened his eyes. She shivered as his hands tightened almost painfully on her hips.

"I have never felt the way I feel now," she said with a gasp. "I can feel a heat from you, a craving, and I want it. I want it all."

His eyes hooded, and she gasped again as he pulled out and shifted down her body. He dipped and sliced his tongue along her slit. His teeth grazed roughly over her aching nub, spiking a deeper desire into her body. He cupped her buttocks in both his palms, tilting her hips and pressing her core to his mouth. His kiss was deep and erotic. He held her under the lash of his tongue, soaking up the hot cries she could not rein in. He feasted, curling his tongue deep inside her, and she spasmed against his mouth.

She rocked against him, wrapped in steaming sensuality, breathless cries echoing from her lips. His teeth closed over her, and she moaned in complete abandon. He nipped her once, twice, three times, then sucked. Her back arched off the bed. Sweat slicked her skin, and desire roared through her. The muscles in her legs strained, she trembled.

Aroused curiosity licked at her consciousness as his fingers trailed her wetness in the crack of her buttocks, rousing nerve endings to life, teasing an entrance she never knew could be touched sexually. She met his wicked gaze and his slow smile had her shaking in need.

He brought his hands down sharply on her center, ripping a wail of tormented pleasure from her. Her mind hazed in shock at the savage feeling of lust that tore through her at the stinging slap that vibrated through her core. She jerked at the delicious friction, at the landing of a second slap.

"There are so many things I want to do to you," he growled, hot lust firing in his eyes. "Things society does not approve of."

Dark, dangerous need rose in her, and shivers of unending sensation racked her. She hadn't known lust could be so powerful, so all-consuming, and she dripped with want. "You know how I feel about their rules."

"I do, thank God."

He parted her thighs, mounting her again, and plunged inside her in one quick, hard movement. Her lips opened but no sound escaped. Her breath strangled and her flesh burned as she adjusted to the thick invasion of his body into hers.

"Anthony," she moaned.

He leaned in, sinking deeper, drawing a guttural moan from her. His fingers curled around her wrists, drawing them up around his neck.

"Hold on," he commanded, her only warning as his hips recoiled and slammed home.

She cried out at the overwhelming sensation. He held her gaze, refusing to release her, and began to ride her in a deep, hard, beautiful rhythm. It was ecstasy, the most nerve-racking pleasure she had ever felt. She writhed beneath him, hips arching, craving to get closer.

She clasped his shoulders; her head thrashed. Her teeth sank deep into his biceps as exquisite sensations sliced through her body. He changed the angle of his thrust so he drove against her knot of pleasure. Her muscles clenched in desperation, and the need for something more fired in her.

"Anthony, more!" she cried. The pleasure was immense, consuming her control. She was tethered on a precipice of pleasure so intense it bordered on pain. He slammed harder, deeper.

And then she screamed, splintered, and fell.

A relentless need burned Anthony's eyes upon seeing her walls completely shattered. She couldn't stop the whimpers and moans that burst raggedly from her lips. He groaned with each whimper, with each of her nips and bites, when she clenched and bathed his length in her pleasure. He arched her hips higher, and drove into her with even more hunger.

She exploded again, screaming and bucking into his thrusts, and he did not stop.

"Again," he snarled.

He opened her wider to his thrusts, and she wrapped her legs higher around the middle of his back. Again ravenous desire filled her, and she sank into it. He drowned her in pleasure. He took her lips roughly; his hips thrust harder with every stroke. He swallowed her renewed cries, her second surrender, and held her tight as she trembled and spasmed. Then his orgasm hit, surrounding her, enveloping her, more powerful than anything she had ever felt, and a savage roar tore from him as their releases merged.

Chapter Twelve

Phillipa awoke slowly, her senses alive. Her skin tingled, and an erection prodded her from behind. The embers from the fire in the hearth barely sparked in the dimly lit bedroom. She started to turn and face Anthony but his hand stilled her. She remained on her side curved into his heat. He eased one of his legs between hers, and a finger probed at her core.

She winced. She felt sore. She bit her lower lip as he started to push into her. His hand snaked across her waist and delved through her curls. His thumb gently circled, and languorous pleasure swept through her body, making her flesh more pliant.

He forged in deep and sure, hips rolling to the rhythm of the rain that pattered against the windows. She should be cold with the fire dying in the room, but she burned. The pleasure was softer, sweeter than it had been over the past few hours in his arms. One hand caressed her breast, with fingers teasing her nipple, while the other remained rubbing her pleasure spot. With a final push, he sheathed himself to the hilt inside her.

"*Mmm…*" she murmured.

"Feel how hot and incredibly slick you are," he muttered at her ear, his voice husky with arousal. "I love your sensuality, your passion, how wet you get for me." He pressed a kiss against the base of her neck, soothing and arousing at the same time.

She whimpered, unsure how he knew. Even though so gentle, he went deep, and her core ached for him. His hip surged, and he picked up a rhythm that had her body weeping with delight. Sweat slicked their skin, and she gasped as he shifted his legs between hers, widening her a little farther, sinking deeper still.

She groaned, trembled, and pressed into his heat that curved behind her so deliciously. Hours seemed to pass as he rode her in the darkened bedchamber. He never increased his tempo and the heat spiraled slower, but was vicious in its intensity. Her release swept over her, scorching in its immensity.

He gently pulled out from her, her flesh almost unwilling to let him go. He was still hard and he shifted, adjusting himself.

"Are you not going to…?"

"No, I am contented." He lifted her hair from her shoulders and pressed a soft kiss to her shoulder.

"Are you sure?"

"Phillipa, I know you are sore after our excessive night."

She still wanted to please him, but she knew he was correct. He'd already loved her four times, and her thighs and inside her ached, and her flesh felt incredibly tender.

"Is there no other way to please you?" she asked.

"I am pleased. Sleep," he ordered.

She thought about it, her brows furrowing in concentration. "When you place your mouth between my legs, I felt waves of pleasure. Would it be the same for you if I took you in my mouth?"

"Hell!" His muscles went rigid around her.

The idea unfurled within her and a smile bloomed. He said nothing save his curse, but he went harder behind her.

She turned and shrugged off the sheets. His eyes hooded, and she grinned. He did not stop her removing the coverlet. Fascination held her as she thought about him feeling as aroused as she did when he kissed her there. For the long night he'd been the one in control. He had kissed, licked, and pleasured her in ways that left her limp but always wanting more. And he'd always given her what she needed.

Now it was her turn.

Phillipa skimmed her hands over his firm abdomen, loving his body. His stomach and chest were rigidly sculpted. His body was beautiful. She kissed his stomach, reveling in his strength and heat. Anthony's erection stood heavy and hard. She had thought to kiss his lips, neck, and body as he did hers, but instead she went straight for his length. She shimmied down, her hands resting against his muscular thighs. They bunched, and she felt pleased that he anticipated her touch.

Oh, yes. This would be as pleasurable for her as it was for him.

Phillipa licked him, a slow, sensuous glide that had Anthony's stomach rippling. A groan slipped from him as he savored the wet heat of her mouth on his cock. Her hands fluttered to his chest, and she reared up as she touched and learned him. He inhaled deeply, to restrain his need, so he would give her all the time she needed to indulge her pleasures. And his.

She started tentative, curious. He watched, enthralled by the heated sensuality that darkened her eyes. Her tongue stroked over the broad head of his erection, and she suckled him slowly. She released it from her mouth with a wet, sucking sound, and he groaned.

Her lips trailed down the rigid length. His balls ached, and he almost shouted as her wet tongue caressed them. She noted his reaction and her feminine smile of lasciviousness enraptured him. She was bloody perfect. With his reaction guiding her, she licked his balls in broad, wet sweeps. Lust shivered into him and tingled up to the tip of his cock, flexing it. Her hair cascaded over her face, obscuring his view, and he gripped it, wrapping it around his hand.

Hell. He was drowning in the wet heat of her mouth. She scorched him with her carnality and beguiled him with the innocent greed she took him with.

With innate instinct, she released him from her mouth and crawled on top of him. Her body swayed with lush eroticism, and she straddled him with her hips. She straightened, and her hair rippled from his hand in fiery tresses.

She stole his breath.

Her nether curls glistened, and wetness seeped along her inner thighs. She gripped him in her hand, and he saw no reserve as she held his gaze and slowly sank onto him.

She glowed warm and vibrant. And he knew she would match him as a lover in all ways. He knew she must be sore, but she was enjoying her sensuality too much, in the wicked lust that arced between them, to stop. No one had ever taken him with such raw, unmatched passion. And that was what she did—she took him, as surely as he had taken her last night. He was mesmerized. And he gave full control over to her.

She bit her lips and bore down inexorably on him. Sliding up and down until she sat boldly astride him, fully seated to the hilt. And then she rode him.

She rode with guilelessness, with sheer wantonness, and with a freedom that utterly captivated him, and he tumbled with her when she fell.

At last, he had met a woman who would match his needs.

Finally, a woman who had captured his heart.

...

Phillipa snuggled into the warmth of Anthony's embrace, unable to move. He drew the coverlet over them when she shivered. The silence between them was comfortable, and she smiled in the darkness, filled with contentment. "Thank you."

"My pleasure," he said, and they both laughed softly.

He pressed another kiss at her nape. "Are you ready to talk about it? About this secret you hold so close?"

His calm question surprised her, but didn't upset her. If he had demanded or berated, she would have retreated behind her usual wall of doubt. But his air of relaxed curiosity made her want to answer. She wanted no more secrets between them.

"I had a lover in Boston," she said softly. "We were childhood friends, and the older I grew the more curious I became about everything. Especially between men and women." She turned into Anthony's arms, needing to see his face. He shifted so he sprawled on his back. She did not resist the arms that drew her down, so that she lay in the crook of his embrace.

"We were best of friends, more than anything else. He introduced me to small adventures. He taught me how to swim in the lakes that I'd been forbidden from, how to ride astride. We were so close it grew into more than friendship. We shared our first kiss together, then more, and eventually our explorations led to us making love."

She inhaled. Brandon had been her first in everything. First bloom of love, first tentative kiss, and when she discovered her parents intended to uproot her from her known world to move to London, she gave herself to him. It had been sweet, painful, a little messy, and very poignant.

"It was more out of defiance than real love, hoping that my parents would leave me behind to wed him. Brandon and

I made grand plans together of where we would travel and what we'd explore. They were more my dreams than his. He knew I wanted to see the world, so he urged me to go with my parents, promising to follow by my twenty-first birthday."

"What happened on your twenty-first birthday?"

"Nothing yet. I'm still only twenty. When I turn twenty-one, I will claim the inheritance my grandmother left me. I planned that we would use it to tour the continents." She twined her fingers through Anthony's. The slow, steady beat of his pulse reassured her.

"Go on," he encouraged.

"My family made me feel so ashamed. I endured Papa slapping me, calling me a harlot, and my mother's wrenching sobs. Mama drew the curtains as if there had been a death in our family, and all she spoke about was the shame. Never mind that the person who had seen us together was Mama herself."

Anthony's hand rubbed her shoulders soothingly.

"By the time we reached London, I felt suffocated under their guilt and expectations. All I heard was how I'd ruined myself and my chances of ever being loved. My aunt tried to arrange a suitable match for my hand. She introduced me to Lord Orwell."

Anthony's muscles tensed. "I assume he presented himself as charming, elegant, wealthy, and everything a young lady ought to dream of in a husband," he drawled.

"Indeed. And my aunt kept singing his praises. I admitted that I found him likable. I attended the opera with him, took early morning rides, and even went on several picnics. My father invested heavily in several of his ventures, to strengthen the connection. After two months of courtship, Orwell made an offer for my hand."

"Even though I had a desperate desire to travel, I was tempted. But I found it distressing to accept a man's proposal, knowing I'd already had a lover. Believing him to be a gentleman, someone I could trust, I confided in him. I told him about Brandon." She cringed, remembering his violent reaction. His hands around her throat and his cruel taunts.

Anthony made a growling noise. "I can only imagine his anger."

"He turned ugly. I instantly ceased to be a lady to him. I realized then that everyone would feel the same way. My own family insisted I was impure. Orwell made me feel much worse." She closed her eyes as the awful memories swept over her.

Anthony's muscles grew even more rigid. "What did the blackguard do?"

"He kissed me. For the first time. Then he made promises of the lavish lifestyle I would live, and how he would provide for me. It took a few minutes to dawn on me that he wanted to establish me as his mistress. I was no longer suitable for marriage. I was soiled goods and could only be his mistress. I said no."

"And he didn't take kindly to your rejection." Anthony's arms tightened around her.

She lay silent for a few minutes, feeling safe, truly protected, for the first time since leaving Boston. "He became a nightmare after that. He hounded me at every turn. He accosted me at balls, trying to force kisses. He said if I did not come to him, he would let it be known I'm a harlot. He would not relent. He resorted to using my father's heavy investments in his schemes as blackmail. He threatened to tell his wealthy friends my father was not an honest man to work with, ruining his business. I was terrified. I needed to escape the vile blackguard. So, I devised a plan."

Anthony peered down at her with a scowl. "What plan?"

"I wrote Brandon to remind him of his promise. But he replied that he'd gotten married. I should have been devastated, but truthfully I was more annoyed my plans had been foiled. So, I resolved to travel alone instead, with a paid companion. My twenty-first birthday is in a couple days." She sighed and fell into the daydreams that had sustained her over the past difficult months. "So, you see? My inheritance will let me leave London and do as I wish. I shall tour the continents and have as many adventures as possible. When I marry, it shan't be to someone from London's *haute monde*."

Anthony's body had grown still beneath her. "Yes. I see."

She stifled a yawn, exhaustion draining her. "I foolishly believed I could ignore Orwell's advances until then. I never imagined that he would kidnap me. I was so afraid." She glanced up at him with a smile. "And then my gallant knight rode up on his white horse and rescued me."

"Odin is black," Anthony said evenly.

She snuggled deeper into his embrace. After last night, his sensual touch had replaced the fear and distaste of Orwell's. Anthony's easy acceptance of her impurity still left her stunned. She instinctively knew he would not hold her in contempt, even now, after she'd confessed everything. "By the way, how *did* you know I was abducted?"

"I had a trail put on you. I was not comfortable with how Orwell hounded you."

"Thank you," she murmured. She probably should be miffed at his arrogant interference. But she wasn't. If not for his concern, her life would now be an unbearable nightmare. If she were alive at all. "I will always be in your debt, Lord Anthony."

Another yawn rushed from her.

"We will continue this discussion later," he said. "Including your debt to me." He shifted her closer, wrapping her in his arms. "But for now, sleep."

It felt perfectly natural, and so right, to place her cheek against the crook of his neck and do as he commanded. And so, she did.

Chapter Thirteen

The lush expanse of Anthony's estate awed Phillipa. The dark green, rolling lushness of the lawns stole her breath. Rows of flowers sprawled in majestic beauty, surrounded by perfectly trimmed hedges. Dozens of elm trees lined the stately driveway. Several French gardens were scattered about in wild disarray, completing the charming effect. In the light of day, what had seemed like a large manor house was in fact an elegant mansion.

Upon rousing, she had slipped from the bed, grateful to see her clothes stitched, ironed, and laid out for her. Then heat had seared her entire body realizing that the maid must have seen her wrapped in Anthony's arms.

After a long, warm bath, she had made her way down the massive hallway and winding staircase, to the sunroom where the butler directed her. It was aptly named, facing east where the sun rose, with an entire wall of windows. The yellow, green, and silver decor of the room was stunning in its elegance, and yet, the room invited comfort.

Footmen had paraded in with eggs, bacon, cheese, cakes,

and tea, to fill the sideboard. But it was the fragrant aroma of coffee that had roused her from her worrying thoughts. She had queried the footman, and had been pleased to have recognized the heady roasted scent of Jamaican blue mountain coffee, a favorite of hers.

She'd eaten her fill and waited with a feeling akin to dread for Anthony to descend. The beauty of his property could not soothe the riotous emotions that jangled inside her. Joy that he had made love to her without disdain. She felt no shame at her own part in their bed play. Though she blushed recalling all the ways he had taken her. She had never expected that making love could be so tumultuous, so delicious.

Where was he? Doubt and worry gnawed at her.

She rose, and tentatively wandered through the mazelike main level of the house. In a small, bright room, she found an easel positioned in front of the windows facing the gardens. She picked up a bit of charcoal. She'd always had an artistic bent, so she sat down before the easel and started to sketch. Her hands slashed with bold movements, and before long, the raw beauty that was Anthony appeared on the paper. She drew him as how she saw him—vital, energetic, and a little rakish. On a whim, she added wings that arched with graceful power on his back. She brushed the charcoal, her brows frowning in intense concentration as she darkened his wings, turning them a deep shade of midnight.

"You are immensely talented."

She gasped in surprise and spun on the stool to look at him. A blush heated her cheeks. She was not sure how to act after their night of excess. "Thank you. I love drawing and painting."

"A lady of many talents." His lips fleetingly brushed against hers, and pleasure unfurled inside of her. He cupped her cheeks, and his thumb caressed a light bruise at the corner of her lips.

"I will crush him," he avowed. "He will not escape unscathed after such contemptible behavior."

Her heart beat faster as he gently kissed the bruise. "Forget him. I don't want him to spoil the day for us."

"You're right. He's forgotten."

She smiled up at him. "Your estate is beautiful."

"Thank you. Come. I have not yet eaten."

They returned to the breakfast room, and he strode to the sideboard, while she accepted another cup of coffee. He filled his plate and she tried not to gape at the quantity when he seated himself across from her and picked up his fork.

"My mother and sister have arrived," he said. "My mother penned a letter to your father, informing your family of your visit, and the rain that forced your overnight stay. No one knows she and my sister only arrived this morning, and it must be kept that way. Many will still speculate, and rumors will abound, since I resided under the same roof. I will announce our engagement, and then we will wait an appropriate time and wed."

Phillipa tilted her head up a notch, filling with rebellion. After telling him of her inheritance last night, she'd been hoping he would dispense with that line of thinking. "If your mother stands behind our tale, such a noble sacrifice on your part is unnecessary."

"It is no sacrifice," he said evenly. "I am happy for us to wed."

She rose from the chair and started to pace. "But I am not."

"Is marriage to me so undesirable?" he asked with a shade of irritation. Or perhaps hurt.

"It is not you, Anthony," she said softly. "It just that…I do not wish to remain in London. I hate the whirl, the restrictions, and the quick condemnation. I am continuously told how a proper young lady must behave. Be biddable, do not prattle, and heaven forbid I display some modicum of intelligence. If our relationship becomes known, I will be ostracized. Better to leave now. I do not need the approval of a society I loathe, and have no intention of spending my life bowing and scraping to it."

She stopped pacing, and sank back into her chair, trying to hold his gaze. His mien was carefully neutral, but she could see the coldness encasing his eyes.

"You know how I feel about marriage," she pleaded. "I hate the condemnation I see blazing from you. Is it not enough that we are lovers?"

He rose and strode around to stand over her. "Is that all you desire of me? For me to be between your legs pleasuring you?" His face was bland, but she thought he sounded a little hurt.

She winced at his bluntness. "No. I enjoy your company. I love being with you—conversing with you, dancing with you. You are the most honorable man I have ever met, but I have no desire for marriage, Anthony. I would like for us to remain lovers and friends."

His chuckle held no mirth as he folded his arms and walked over to lean against the mantel. "You do not understand the nature of the society you live in, Phillipa. This is about more than us being lovers. Orwell will undoubtedly drop hints about you, providing grist for the vicious rumor mill. He is a coward and will never act in an honorable manner. You can only benefit from our marriage."

She clamped her jaw. Why did everyone insist they knew better than she what would benefit her? Still, the last thing she wanted was to fight with Anthony. Not after all the wondrous things they had shared together. She slowly took a few sips of coffee, composing her thoughts, trying to still the trembling of her heart.

"What benefit will being married provide to me?

Pleasure? I can receive pleasure without tying myself to the whims of a man. A man who can dictate how I dress, what I do, a man who can beat me any time he so wishes. I want to travel. Africa, Egypt, Shanghai, the Caribbean. You propose to be my husband, Anthony. Will you be content with a wife who is not here, attending to you and your home? Will you be content with a wife who yearns for more than a conventional life, instead of one who gives you babies and hosts your dinner parties? A wife who will attend women's rights conventions?" She hiked a brow. "I don't think that is what you want in a wife."

His face shuttered, and her heart squeezed. For some reason she desperately wanted him to say yes, he did. He wanted her with all her eccentric ways. *Because* of all her eccentric ways.

"You paint quite a picture," he ground out.

"You seek to marry me out of some misguided notion of chivalry, Anthony. I'm telling you, it is not necessary."

"I do not offer to marry out of honor or to obtain legal issue," he growled.

"Why then? Love?" She scoffed, expecting it to be anything but. Her heart shook when she noticed his expression closed up even further.

Love?

"Much too high an aspiration for a licentious rake such as myself," he bit out coldly. He stalked to the window and thrust his hands deep into his pockets.

Phillipa hesitated, then got to her feet and went to him. "You know very well I did not mean it like that, Anthony. You are not debauched in any way. You are both heroic and kind. I simply have no desire to wed, and I do not understand why we must do so if your mother will help us avoid a scandal."

He shifted, and she held his gaze. Her chest squeezed as his eyes became even more distant. Concern curled inside her.

He lifted his hand, and his thumb brushed against her lips, slowly, seductively. The regret that coated his voice deepened her unease. "The bonds of matrimony are never something I would enter lightly, nor for something as cold as chivalry. But I understand now, that is all you would see them as, Phillipa. *Bonds*." He dropped his hand and gave a curt bow, conceding to her wishes.

She did not feel the relief she had expected to feel. Instead, her stomach felt hollow. Confusion swirled through her, and she hated the blank, neutral look that evened out his features as he walked back to the table.

"Anthony." She was afraid to ask, but she needed to know. "Are we still lovers?"

He sat back down, methodically finishing his food. "I am not interested in a cold, meaningless relationship, Phillipa. If I need sex, I can take a mistress. I want more. A wife…children, a family."

"What we have is not cold and meaningless!" she said, affront tingeing her words. "You knew how I felt. Did you think I would change my mind after spending one night in your bed?"

His expression didn't flicker. "My mother and Constance will travel with you back to London. She will tell your family, and anyone else who asks, that you dined with us and the inclement weather prevented your return. Hopefully, that will be enough to silence the gossips."

Phillipa nodded mutely at his matter-of-fact recitation, dropping her gaze to her hands and swallowing the lump that had formed in her throat. She was suddenly hit by a painful realization. If he had murmured words of affection, or love, rather than cold logic, she might actually have considered marriage.

But it was too late now. Pride tied her tongue. If Anthony had felt affection for her, he would have said so when she mentioned love. She would not mistake the passion between them to mean anything deeper to him than lust.

His mother swept into the breakfast room, and Phillipa blinked at her dainty perfection. She forced herself not to react to the curious way the viscountess regarded her. She must know Phillipa spent the night with her son.

Anthony's voice remained blandly polite as he introduced them.

She battled the urge to fidget. Or smack him for his damned insouciance. Instead, she curtsied nicely. "My lady."

His mother's nod of acknowledgement was regal, and her warm smile banished some of the tension from Phillipa's body.

A sigh came from Anthony at a ruckus that sounded from the hallway. The door was flung open, and a young lady barreled into the room. She blazed in without decorum, running past Phillipa to fling herself at him for a hug. He grunted as if annoyed, but he returned her embrace, kissing her cheek.

"Oh, Anthony, he is bloody fabulous. I cannot believe he is all mine!"

"Constance!" Lady Radcliffe's admonishment had her spinning around laughing.

Phillipa was stunned by Lady Constance's beauty. She was a replica of Anthony's blond looks, with his same sparkling green eyes. She possessed the petite body of her mother, except her curves were richly pronounced.

"Oh, Mother! Anthony has planned to gift me with a horse sired from Odin for my birthday, and I have just ridden him, though he won't officially be mine for six more weeks. He is so divine, and I am so thrilled!"

"I see I will have to relieve the stable master of his duties," Anthony drawled.

"Oh, rubbish. He could not very well refuse to answer

when I demanded to know whose horse it is."

"Lady Constance, may I present Miss Phillipa Peppiwell. Miss Peppiwell, my sister."

Lady Constance's energy whirled toward Phillipa, and she clapped enthusiastically. "Oh! A second gift! I am most pleased to meet you, Miss Peppiwell."

Phillipa gazed at her with a slight frown. "As am I—"

"I do *so* hope you will teach me how to ride astride. Tongues have been wagging in the drawing rooms at your boldness, Miss Peppiwell. I think it's grand, and you are very brave, indeed."

"Well, I—" Phillipa winced at the appalled look Lady Radcliffe gave her daughter. Anthony looked on with a sort of brotherly indulgence, but she got the distinct feeling he would lock his sister up for a year if she actually dared to ride astride.

"Please ignore my daughter's rudeness, Miss Peppiwell. She has yet to understand that a young lady does not behave in such a manner."

Phillipa nodded blandly, refusing to rise to the implication that she was, therefore, clearly not a lady. She was quite used to such thoughtless statements, and far from being offended, was secretly pleased by the characterization.

The rest of the morning passed in a blur of friendly chatter and preparation for travel. When Phillipa departed, Anthony placed a perfunctory kiss on her cheek that had his mother smiling. Whether from the kiss itself, or from his cool politeness, Phillipa wasn't certain.

In any case, she steadfastly refused to beg a private audience with him, and bundled herself into the viscountess's carriage without any further discussion of their relationship.

The trip to London was uneventful. Phillipa felt the palpable curiosity of Lady Constance and Lady Radcliffe, but instead of prying, they filled the journey with mild pleasantries and inane chatter about balls, mutual acquaintances, and the weather. Phillipa found herself liking them both very much. She answered their polite inquires about her family graciously, happy they confined their questions mainly to her sisters.

On the inside, her feelings were riotous. Anthony had not seemed angry, but he'd been distant with her, to the point of coldness. She clenched her hands on her lap, despising the uncertainty in her mind…and her heart. Had she made the right decision, refusing his offer?

What a tangle her life had suddenly become.

Phillipa was more than grateful for Lady Radcliffe's aid in her current situation, and quietly told her so before facing her father. But as it turned out, her return home was without fanfare or the upset she had feared. Her aunt had received a note last night from the viscountess informing of Phillipa's stay, so no one had worried. Rather than being distressed, Lady Merryweather was visibly pleased to know she'd spent the night at Lord Anthony's home. After an hour of afternoon tea and lively conversation with her mother and aunt, the viscountess and Lady Constance departed.

Phillipa's aunt wasted no time in pouncing on her. "This is wonderful news, Phillipa! Lord Anthony's mother has taken quite a shine to you. You can expect his courtship to begin at once."

"It will be in vain. I still do not wish to marry," she assured her, wondering briefly at the lack of conviction in her voice.

"Nonsense," her mother declared. "I have complete confidence that you will see the immense benefit to your father of connecting with such an esteemed family. Payton has also made a wonderful match, and I am very proud both my girls will be wed by next season. Payton will be the Lady Jenson St. John, and you Lady Anthony Thornton, and perhaps a duchess one day."

Phillipa hated the tiny thrill that went through her at the

idea of being Anthony's lady. She prayed he had not really ended their association. She was not sure if that was what he'd done. But the pain that clawed through her heart at the mere possibility was almost unbearable.

She retired early, drained from the entire ordeal. She sank into slumber, resolved to determine if Anthony felt affection for her.

For she had finally cast aside her doubt, and admitted to herself that if he felt even a sliver of affection that could grow to love, she would marry him.

Her grandmother always said that any man who loved her, while he held her heart in the palm of his hands, she held his soul in the heart of hers, and he would give her all she desired.

Chapter Fourteen

Three days had passed since Phillipa departed Anthony's estate with his mother and sister. And three endless nights. He was now visiting with Lady Jocelyn in Lincolnshire. It should have taken his mind from Phillipa, but seeing Lady Jocelyn again only reaffirmed Phillipa had ruined him for any other woman. Because he was still as tormented today as he'd been the first night.

Anthony asked himself for the fifth time why he was in the woods of Stone Haven hunting with Lady Jocelyn. *Hunting*. Another unorthodox female in his life. The second female he knew who rode so boldly astride without fear of society's disapproval. She was now dressed in boy's pants and was far too comfortable with her bow and arrow.

She smiled over her shoulder at him and he smiled back, following behind on his horse.

Seeing Lady Jocelyn was a whim he did not regret. It was a relief to know that his polite note had never been delivered to her. She still had the locket, and he'd seen the questions in her eyes, yet so far she'd asked him nothing. He wondered what she would say if he truly unburdened and told her of his illegitimacy and Phillipa's rejection of his proposal.

Lady Jocelyn was glad to see him, but it was not the happiness of a missed lover. He doubted she even saw him as a man. *Hell*. How she looked at him actually reminded him of how his mother had been with the old duke. He'd never seen them kiss or even touch, never seen any passion or joy between them. He'd only seen his mother's misery and the tears she'd thought she shed in secret.

Even so, if he ever wed Lady Jocelyn, he doubted they would have such a cold marriage. He liked her. Her fierceness he had never encountered in another woman, and her warmth was captivating. It was a pity he could not feel anything deeper for her, but at least they would have friendship, a thing many marriages lacked. Ironically, when he'd resolved to find a bride, the only requirement he'd really had was that they love each other. He scoffed. His brother may really be right. Love was an unrealistic ideal he was chasing.

"*Shhh*, my lord." She smiled and pressed a finger to her lips. "You are being too noisy. We are going to scare them away."

His eyes slid over the curve of her rump so clearly outlined in her tightly fitting breeches. He shook his head, disappointed when nothing stirred within him.

"You seem distracted today," she remarked.

He grimaced. "I do have some unresolved issues in London. Forgive me."

"Do you want to talk about it?" she asked with a warm smile.

"I do not." He smiled to remove the sting. "My visit was meant to clear my head of my troubles. Tell me of the irrigation system you want to implement here at Stone Haven."

The restoration of her home, a topic dear to her, had the desired effect, and with dizzying animation she launched into her dreams for her home.

They dismounted and walked through the woods while chatting softly, and he cursed his mind for constantly turning to Phillipa.

Lady Jocelyn frowned at his inattentiveness. "Are you certain you do not wish to speak of your troubles, my lord?"

"Thank you for your concern, but I am certain."

There was a rustle and she placed a finger to her lips for silence and crept steadily ahead, bow and arrow angled skillfully. He watched her as she raised her bow in perfect position and sighted the hare. But the arrow missed.

"Bloody hell!"

And she also cursed. He smiled at her scrunched face.

"I am not in fit shape today, Lord Anthony. I think we must leave hunting for another day," she said on a laugh, tucking her bow away.

They exited the woods and swung onto their horses.

Lady Jocelyn glanced at him. "Are you here for the locket, my lord?"

He chuckled. The lady was really forthright. But why *was* he there? He'd only wanted to put some space between himself and Phillipa. To remain in the manor where they had made love, where he could see her beside him always, was slow torture. "No. That was not the thought that drove me here."

Her shoulders relaxed slightly. "I see. Your distraction in London?"

The lady was perceptive, as well.

He nodded, wanting to be honest with her without divulging too much.

"Would you like me to keep the locket until you have solved whatever put such a faraway look in your eyes? Or would you like me to return it?" she asked him bluntly.

He grinned in admiration. No wilting miss, this one.

"Keep the locket until I return from London. Then we will speak further about it."

"*Hmm*. In that case, I think I must know about this distraction," she drawled teasingly.

Anthony laughed at her impudence. "Not a chance."

"Well, then. Let us race!"

Before he could respond, she urged her mount into a gallop, and welcoming the freedom of the challenge, he raced after her. Admiration filled him as she rode ahead. The lady was bold and fearless, yet so charming. He knew the woman in front of him would make him a good wife and he should commit to her. She understood her role in London's *haute monde*. She had no desire to roam the continents, traipsing over the world and eating French desserts for breakfast. She did not desire total freedom. She *wanted* to get married.

Yet, it was only Phillipa he could see beside him, swollen with his child, reposing on the lawn reading.

Swollen with child. Bloody hell.

He almost toppled from his horse as the possibility roared through him. He drew on the reins, slowing the horse to a stop, his mind whirling. He had been so enthralled with Phillipa precautions had never entered his mind. She could even now be carrying his child.

He stilled, fighting the possessive flare that rose in him at the image.

Lady Jocelyn's laughter carried on the wind as she waved her hands in the distance. Yet all that clamored in his mind was that he must go to Phillipa immediately. For he could determine nothing more about his future until he knew for certain she was not enceinte. Certainly, before he could even entertain the idea of offering for Lady Jocelyn.

Though, he feared in his gut if he lost Phillipa fully, it would take him months, perhaps even years before he could court another.

· · ·

Anthony made the decision to follow Phillipa to London. He departed Lincolnshire that same evening. He also wanted to ensure she was safe and well, and that their ruse to circumvent the wagging tongues had worked. And he needed to completely eradicate the threat of Lord Orwell.

He had set Hawke to investigating everything about the man, and had kept several men watching Phillipa with specific orders of how they should deal with a threat to her person. All reports he had received so far indicated that Orwell was keeping a careful distance from her, hiding in his town house, no doubt nursing his wounds…and his wounded ego.

Which was a good thing. Anthony would not be responsible for his actions if Orwell so much as came within shouting distance of Phillipa.

Despite the danger of provoking speculation by the gossips, he needed to see her. He missed her with every part of his being.

Memories of their lovemaking slid into his dreams, and he wondered if he would ever be free of the physical need he felt for her. He had never been captivated by a woman as much as he was by her. She was the most exciting lover he had ever possessed, but he wanted her for more than her breathtaking sensuality.

He admired the strength she had displayed in the face of Orwell's atrocities. He was amazed by her certainty of will and craving to determine her own fate. Her intelligence, wit, and curiosity astounded him. There was much about her that appealed to him on a deep level.

He felt something fiercely for Phillipa, and he was not the kind of man to shy away from his feelings. He wanted to strip her layers bare and understand her better. Though, in truth, what drove her was not so difficult to decipher.

He loved the way her face animated when she spoke of being free from society's strictures. A freedom he yearned for himself, if he would only dare admit it. He would give anything to leave the cares of this life behind him, for the freedom to not worry about his legitimacy—whether it would be revealed, and whether it would one day taint his sons and daughters.

Yes, Anthony understood Phillipa perfectly, the reason she craved freedom, and he found that he wanted to pursue that freedom with her. He'd felt that same need as a youth when faced with the immutable fact of his father's disregard. After finishing at Oxford, Anthony had taken a lengthy Grand Tour, exploring the continents, and life on that epic journey had never seemed more promising. He had been immersed in the very freedom Phillipa spoke of.

And now he wanted to show her all the sights and wonders he had enjoyed so much, especially Egypt. The lush, exotic beauty of those lands had filled him with a deep and visceral appreciation of nature. He wanted her to experience that, too, and he wanted her to experience it with him.

But he knew he could never be so irresponsible as to flaunt the rules of society and sail away with Phillipa on the adventures she craved. He would not leave Constance to face such an uncertain future. Or his mother, for that matter.

Why the hell should it matter to anyone but the immediate family that his mother had a lover with whom she'd borne two children? Private affairs should never have such power to crush and devastate.

He wanted Phillipa in his life. Permanently. And he wanted her in a way that would not excite the censure of Society. That would bring with it too great a possibility for disaster and devastation for his entire family.

They needed to marry. And marry quickly.

But he was damned if he knew how to convince her to accept his offer. Perhaps if he tempted her with her dreams…

He wanted so much more from her than to be her partner in adventure, but he would start with that…and pray in time she would come to love him. If she was still adamant against marriage, he would leave and resign himself to marrying elsewhere…eventually.

He wagered Phillipa would ask to remain as his lover. But that he would not do. He would not risk getting her with his child, bringing it into the world with the stain of illegitimacy, like himself.

If she continued to refuse his offer, he would respect her wishes. But only after he was certain she did not carry his child.

...

He'd come for her!

With a rush of nervous excitement, Phillipa watched Anthony's dark blond head as he scanned the crowded ballroom. She prayed it was she that he sought.

The past few days had been agonizing; she'd fretted constantly, wondering if she had made the right decision. She had warred with her own needs, going back and forth in her mind.

Freedom and adventure…or to have forever the man she had come to love.

An impossible choice.

More than anything, she wished to escape her mother and aunt and their insistence on all that a proper young lady encompassed. Yet, her traitorous heart had whispered that to be shackled to Lord Anthony would mean a life of unending adventure and delight.

She'd missed him terribly. She had only known him for a few weeks, yet had such a depth of feelings for him, it felt as though they'd been together for a lifetime.

Thankfully, upon her return to London, Orwell seemed to have disappeared. And she had not detected any hint or whisper of his despicable actions or the fact that she'd spent a night at Anthony's house in Baybrook. She'd attended a soiree last night, and tonight a ball, basking in her sister's happiness at being engaged to Lord Jensen St. John. Certainly an affable young fellow, and her sister glowed with adoration whenever she spoke of him.

But every moment, Phillipa had watched for Anthony, hoping he would attend and seek her out.

A sharp ache sliced through her as she followed his progress up the stairs toward her. Oh, how she'd missed him!

Tonight he wore a dark tailcoat with the most dashing pearly white waistcoat, complemented by an immaculately tied white cravat. A ripple of goose bumps danced over her skin the moment he spied her. His eyes devoured her, from her soft pink gown, elaborately coifed hair, and the lace shawl that hung loosely on her bare elbows. His gaze lingered on her breasts, her waist, and finally her lips. She tingled in anticipation.

"Do you think he will come this way?"

She did not take her eyes off him at Elisabeth's whispered question. Dozens of people stopped him, and he did not shrug them off, taking long, frustrating minutes to socialize. Yet she saw he kept her in his sight at all times.

"I do not know. He has not sent word for three whole days."

Elisabeth stared at her in amusement. "Really? So long?"

Phillipa sent her a withering glare. "I'm a fool, I know, but it seems like a lifetime."

She had ached for him, even wept tears, tormented with the need she'd felt for him, both physically and in her mind. She had started to accept that she loved him. And it had felt right. Until doubts assailed her.

If he had felt even a sliver of affection for her, how

could he have been so withdrawn when she left him? And so tellingly silent for the past few days?

Had Anthony changed his mind about marriage to her, and accepted her refusal?

She wasn't an easy handful. She knew that. Perhaps he'd felt only relief that he'd been so easily rid of her.

She took the glass of champagne Elisabeth pressed in her hand and tried to ignore the wild thumping in her heart. She had never expected to long for him the way she had.

The past few nights had been tormented with memories and dreams of their lovemaking. In the days she had yearned to be with him. She had longed to converse with him, to share the plans she had for her future. *Their* future.

He had also missed her birthday celebration earlier this evening. Not that it had been so grand. Only a small dinner gathering of family and a few friends, but she had foolishly sent him an invitation to his town house. She'd also invited Lady Constance and Lady Radcliffe, and her aunt and mother had been thrilled with their presence. Phillipa had been too embarrassed to ask about Anthony's whereabouts, and his mother and sister had not volunteered any hints.

She had forced herself not to dwell on him. But more and more she kept hoping that Anthony would come for her. Or at least send a polite note. She'd needed to know if they were to be friends, or nothing at all.

Phillipa narrowed her eyes as he finally turned his full attention upon her. He prowled across the room toward her. She loved the untamed rawness he vibrated with. She composed her features into a neutral mask, praying he did not think to cut her after she had rejected him.

"Lady Elisabeth." He greeted Elisabeth with a curt bow. He did not remove his eyes from Phillipa's, and after a low acknowledgement, Elisabeth disappeared into the crowd.

Phillipa's breath hitched at what she saw in his eyes.

Hunger. Her heart stuttered in the most painful rhythm, and emotion tightened her throat. Her hands trembled and he pried her grip from the champagne glass and handed it to a servant who scurried over with a silver tray.

He did not speak, simply put her arm though his and led her away. She felt she should discreetly look to see who observed them, but the weakness that swept through her prevented any action on her part except to obey.

As they walked through the crowd, he paused to respond to a few people. He maneuvered them toward the card room. Instead of entering, he took her farther down the hallway. They passed the Dewitt's massive library, then the parlor, and then with a quick look around, he led her upstairs. They walked down the eerily quiet corridor.

She swallowed, her throat dry, unable to speak, even though words begged to tumble from her lips. He opened a door and drew her in. The darkness swallowed them and her senses heightened. The scent of clean linens reached her nostrils and his own masculine scent.

She had thought to bombard him with questions. Instead, her mind now clouded with desire and conversing was the last thing she wanted to do. Tension and need roiled within her, triggered by the familiar, musky smell of his need for her.

He backed her farther into the small room, until her buttocks met a table. She could barely make out his features in the darkness. Her limbs shook as she lifted her hands to grasp his shoulders.

The soft rasp of his trousers being unbuttoned made a hot bolt of lust drilled through her body. Her knees went weak, and she was instantly aroused for him.

He lifted her and placed her on the table, then kicked her thighs wide apart and stepped between them, bunching her dress up at her waist. Her petticoats crinkled and the material conformed under his will.

Her throat convulsed as his hand reached for her drawers, but found none.

"Still thumbing your nose at the rules, Phillipa?"

"No. Preparing myself for you," she murmured, and for a moment he froze.

Then his finger unerringly found her core. Her cheeks grew hot at the wetness he found without even kissing her. A hiss escaped his lips, and the sudden feel of the broad head of his erection pressed at her entrance.

"Is this what you want?"

An agonizing need for him to fill her encompassed her whole body. "Yes."

"It will be hard and rough." His voice was guttural.

Arousal nearly stole her voice as she whispered into the dark, "Please, Anthony."

He slammed deep into her, forging past her resistance, plunging to the hilt. She slid on the polished wood of the table, and his hands thrust under her buttocks to pull her forward.

"I missed you," he growled. "I dreamed of you. I bloody ached for you."

She held him tight, her heart soaring. "And I for you."

He withdrew his length slowly until he was once again poised at her entrance. He shoved back in hard and deep, wrenching a strangled groan from her throat.

"I resolved to stay away from you, as you wished, but the moment I saw you I had to kiss you, touch you, be inside you." His thickness moved inside her with powerful thrusts, and exquisite tension coiled in her inner muscles.

"Please don't ever stay away again. I missed you so much, Anthony."

His grip tightened on her hips, and pleasure arched up her spine beading her nipples. They stabbed against her corset, and she desperately wanted to free her breasts.

"Not ever?" he growled between plunges.

"Never." She mewled; she was so close. "Ever."

He hammered into her. "What are you saying?"

"Yes, I will." The words wrenched from her, unstoppable.

He dipped his head lower, kissing the corner of her lips. "Yes what, Phillipa?"

"Yes, I will marry you."

His body halted, and he took her lips in a searing kiss. Then it deepened, and grew more passionate, fierce elation exuding from him.

He gripped her hips tighter. "It's going to get rougher. Hold on."

She responded with shivering waves of need. She lifted her legs to circle his hips, crossing her ankles high on his back, and she clasped him tightly. She buried her face against his throat, trembling from the viciousness of the arousal that burned inside her.

He palmed both cheeks of her buttocks, leaning her back on the table so that his weight settled more on her, sinking deeper into her. She pressed a wet, open kiss on the corded muscles of his neck, loving the taste of his skin.

He rasped against her inner walls as he withdrew from her slowly. Anticipation had her filling with wantonness, both dreading and craving the roughness he promised. She screamed into his neck when he slammed home. She drove her fingers into his hair and gripped his head. He rode her rough and hard, peppering kisses against her shoulder and growling out words of encouragement. She luxuriated in his heat, in his powerful maleness, in his strength as he loved her with fierce need. She arched into him as he gave one final thrust, roared his pleasure, and swept them under together.

Afterward, she lay beneath him panting and heart thundering. But never had she felt calmer and more content.

Finally she was at peace, now that she was back in his arms.

Chapter Fifteen

The next morning, Phillipa was deliriously happy. The severe chill from the inclement weather could not douse her jubilant mood. She curled her hands, warming them over the cup of tea her mother handed her. Anthony would speak with her father that afternoon.

She'd been giddy with excitement after their tumultuous lovemaking in the linen closet. They had laughed like idiots after, and she couldn't stop hugging and kissing him. She had whispered fiercely that she still wanted to travel, but she desperately wanted to be his wife, if his offer still stood.

He had hugged her even tighter. "I already have the special license in hand and shall send an announcement to the papers tomorrow."

They had been very circumspect in sneaking back into the ball.

"Are you certain he's coming, my dear?" her mother queried for the tenth time.

"Yes, Mama," she answered.

"But why would he not present himself this morning?

Why the delay, if you've already given him your answer?" Lady Merryweather asked.

For once, Phillipa didn't mind the inquisition. Nothing could spoil her mood today.

"Lord Anthony had some business to attend. He will call on Papa this afternoon." Phillipa tried to rein in her impatience, not wanting their doubt to feed hers.

Just before parting last night, Anthony had told her he wanted a word with her before he spoke with her father. Anthony had seemed so intent he had scared her a little. She'd demanded to know immediately what was wrong, but he had only shaken his head. Phillipa still felt a trickle of unease over his odd behavior, but determinedly pushed it aside. He wanted to marry her. What could possibly be amiss?

A sharp rap on the door, and their butler announced the first of their morning callers—Lord Hoyt and his sister, Lady Henrietta. Phillipa rose and curtsied as they were shown into the drawing room. Lord Hoyt gave her a warm smile before bowing to her aunt and her mother.

Pleasantries were exchanged, but his sister fairly vibrated with eagerness to speak. Phillipa knew that only occurred when Lady Henrietta had some juicy titbit of gossip to impart. The feather hat on her head bobbed in her excitement as she dismissed the offer of tea and cake.

Phillipa really did not want to be a part of this. "I'm afraid I have some pressing correspondence that needs to be answered to urgently," she said, rising to her feet.

"Oh, Phillipa, you'll want to hear the news I have. You must stay." Lady Henrietta's voice was shrilled.

Phillipa restrained a flinch.

Her mother sent her a stern look and reached for the teapot. "Go on, my lady. Tell us." Her mother poured Lord Hoyt a cup of tea and arranged cakes on a plate.

Phillipa set her face in pleasant determination. "I really

must—"

"Lord Anthony Thornton has been exposed as a bastard," Hoyt murmured portentously.

Lady Merryweather gasped. Her mother froze in the act of handing him the cup of tea. Hot liquid sloshed before Lord Hoyt steadied it, wetting the table and pooling liquid on its gleaming surface.

Phillipa dropped abruptly back into her chair. "What?"

The silence in the room pressed in on her.

"Lord Hoyt," Lady Merryweather admonished, though she could not hide the horror in her voice. "What an unkind thing to say!"

Phillipa tried to comprehend the import of what was being said. Her mother looked ready to swoon, and dismay laced her aunt's gaze.

"I assure you, Lady Merryweather," he defended, "it is all that is being talked about in the drawing rooms this morning. We heard it directly from Lady Godey's lips."

"Everyone has noted that Lord Anthony has singled you out of late, Phillipa," Henrietta murmured with false concern. Her smile was tinged with such maliciousness, Phillipa drew back, startled.

Her throat closed in shock. "I—"

"That is why we hastened to you with the news, my dear." Lord Hoyt reached for her hand and she snatched it away from him. Why did he look so satisfied?

"Well, I don't believe it," she said.

He leaned forward eagerly. "Many will start to whisper about your connection with such a vile imposter pretending to be an honorable gentleman. I believe the matter I brought to your attention at Lady Graham's ball must be broached with your father today to avoid embroiling you in scandal, my dear."

Good heavens! Anthony, a vile imposter?

Her aunt surged to her feet, "Oh, Lord Hoyt, what wonderful news. I will alert Mr. Peppiwell that you wish to speak with him."

Phillipa stared at her, aghast. "No!"

"My love," Lord Hoyt began, but she slashed her hands in the air, cutting him off.

She straightened her spine and met his gaze. "I am already engaged to be married to Lord Anthony. Lord Hoyt, I insist you cease from maligning my betrothed's good name."

Lady Henrietta twittered, "Oh, my." She gave her brother a telling look, as if she had warned him.

"My God," her mother cried. "You can't—"

"God has nothing to do with it Mama. These are vicious rumors, and I will not be a part of this discussion!" She shot to her feet. It was vicious gossip, nothing more. Anthony would never have kept such a thing from her. *Would he?*

The look of appalled betrayal on her mother's face had Phillipa immediately regretting her outburst. Even Henrietta had been rendered speechless, and she stared at Phillipa with an expression of amazed horror.

"I'm sorry, Mama. But, surely, you see this cannot be true."

"Think of the humiliation you and your family will have to endure if you go through with this madness." Lord Hoyt spoke gently. "The stain on his name will be irredeemable. People will no longer invest with him and he will be cut socially and you along with him."

"You will *not* align yourself with such a man." Her mother fanned herself frantically, her face mottled with anger, and she looked as though she was working herself up to a swoon.

"Mama, please. There is no need for theatrics."

"Do not be flippant with your mother, Phillipa." Lady Merryweather's spine snapped straight, but her face had gone ashen with a look in her eyes Phillipa could not bear to see.

Her heart thundered. And she'd thought being caught

spending the night in his home would be a scandal!

Society thrived on malicious gossip, and she could only imagine the tidal wave of condemnation that would follow them now. Her stomach roiled, and she fought to keep her face expressionless. *Oh, Anthony!*

"You must listen to reason, my love." Lord Hoyt looked at her with earnest regard and she could see he was sincere. Unlike his sister's vicious glee.

"Surely, this is only a foul rumor," she murmured after a few tense seconds, pacing away from him.

"I am afraid not," Lord Hoyt said bluntly. "You've only to see him standing next to his mother's new husband to know the truth of that relationship."

Her aunt gripped her hands, her eyes lit with sympathy.

"I came to ask for your hand in marriage, Phillipa. My intentions remain the same," Hoyt said, coming to stand beside her.

Phillipa shook her head, unable to form words. She skirted around him, approaching her mother. "Even if it's true, I doubt he will fall to ruin. He is part of one of the wealthiest, most influential families in the highest echelon of society, Mama. I still—"

Her mother slapped her. She recoiled in shock, her head snapping back. "Mother!" She touched her cheek, tears springing to her eyes.

"Do not be foolish," her mother hissed. "He is *not* a Thornton. Calydon will doubtless distance himself from his false brother, and Lord Anthony will be seen by society as nothing but an affront to morality. You will *not* bring shame on this family again, young lady!"

Fury slashed through Phillipa. "We are *betrothed*. How can you demand I beg off because of a vicious rumor?" Her eyes and throat burned with the injustice.

"They are more than rumors, Miss Peppiwell. One only

has to look at Lord Radcliffe and the truth is apparent," Hoyt insisted.

She gaped at him. Then she turned to Lady Merryweather for support. "Aunt Florence, please."

"You must not be selfish, Phillipa," she admonished sharply. "Your actions reflect on all of us. Think of your father. Your sisters. The stain of this would travel with Payton and Phoebe for years to come."

Phillipa thought of the gallant way Anthony had rescued her. His efforts to protect her reputation by offering marriage. The way he made love to her to ensure her pleasure. His charm and kindness and sincerity, his immense popularity among Society, his unabashed love and concern for his sister.

But mostly Phillipa remembered the way he listened to her. With respect and as an equal. He saw everything about her—good and bad—and he did not judge her for any of it. "He is a good man, Aunt, honorable and strong," she insisted tearfully.

"A bastard is a nobody. He is nothing now. He will no longer be accepted in drawing rooms, or be accepted by anyone of consequence. How can you even think to align our family with such a man?" her aunt said coldly.

Phillipa's chest tightened at the heartless statement. Incredulity quickly flared along with her mounting rage. A few weeks ago, Anthony had been the prime catch of the season. Those were the words her aunt herself had used more than once. Now he was nothing? She had always loved her aunt tremendously, but now all she felt was anger and disgust. Never had she hated the fickleness of society more than in this minute.

"Phillipa, please!" She spun at Payton's pain-filled cry. Horror had slackened her sister's face and twisted her hands together.

"Oh, Payton." Tears spilled from Phillipa's eyes.

"If you wed him, St. John will retract his offer." Payton's pained wail slammed into Phillipa as nothing else could have done.

"Payton, if he loves you, surely, he will—"

"He loves me. He has told me so many times." Her voice broke and tears splashed down her face.

Phillipa hurried to her, clasping her trembling fingers. "Payton, I love Anthony. I cannot—"

"Has he declared his love for you? Has he?" Payton demanded.

Phillipa froze, hurt and uncertainty screaming at her insides. Her sister knew he had not. Phillipa had confessed her doubts to Payton the night before while they lay by the fire in her bedchamber, talking about the two men in their lives. They had both glowed with happiness and love.

Payton gripped her hand. "Are you willing to ruin my happiness and fight for a man who does not love you? And a man who says he will speak with Papa for your hand, but had more pressing issues to attend first?"

Phillipa stepped back, shocked at her vehemence. She forgave her instantly, knowing the fear Payton felt. But her words still created a niggle of doubt.

He had *not* whispered words of love. Not once.

"Come here," she whispered, drawing Payton into her arms, hugging her tightly. "All will be well. I'm sure of it."

Phillipa met Lord Hoyt's gaze over Payton's head and gave him an even look. The hopeful pleasure that suffused his face sickened her. She had not accepted his offer, but she had not refused, either. He already felt he had won. She knew she must act out this charade until she could speak with Anthony. But dread filled her whole body, for she did not know if she could marry him if the rumors were true. The scandal would destroy the connections her father hoped to make.

And with a certainty she could no longer shrug off, she

knew they could not be mere rumors. The man she loved was a bastard.

Oh, God, what was she to do?

• • •

The hum of the gentleman's club seemed muted. Anthony sipped his port and read the report on Orwell with a cold distance. The blackguard was financially powerful, enjoying profitable returns from his many investments.

Hawke's report was extensive, but despite that, he'd failed him. Orwell had retired to his country home in Suffolk and disappeared from the watchful eyes of the men Hawke had placed on him. Anthony found it curious that he had vanished without causing any ripples. Thankfully, he had not been sighted near Phillipa.

Anthony came to an entry in the report, and frowned. Orwell had visited his attorney the day before he disappeared. And they shared the same attorney. A chair scraped and his head snapped up to meet Calvert's worried gaze.

Anthony was surprised to see Sebastian was also with him. Anthony leaned back in his chair as they sat, foreboding flooding over him at the look of savage fury on their faces. "What has happened?" he demanded.

"Newport has disappeared. His office was ransacked and all his correspondence missing. I traveled posthaste to let you know," Sebastian said flatly.

Anthony clutched the report in his hand. *Damnation*. There was little doubt what all this meant. "Is Constance safe?"

"She is with our mother. We must go to her immediately."

He nodded in agreement. Constance needed him. A cold, calm logic filled his mind, and he sifted through his options. He slashed his attention to Calvert. "What bad news do you bring me?"

Anthony saw the sympathy in his friend's eyes and braced himself, though he knew what was coming.

"My father and several others were meeting to discuss withdrawing from ventures that you are heavily invested in."

"Which ones?" he demanded.

"The railways and the steam engines."

He calculated the loss, and the shares he had in them. Substantial, but he should survive.

"The reason?" he demanded evenly, needing confirmation of the worst.

"Lord Hubert and the Marquis of Gale report that you are not a legitimate heir to the Calydon holdings. They have refused to continue any business transactions with you. I tried to inform them that to withdraw from you is to withdraw from Calydon completely. They did not seem to agree," Calvert said, anger threading his voice, as well.

Anthony met Sebastian's gaze. They believed his own brother would turn from him, in fear of tainting the Calydon title. A thing he knew would happen when hell froze over.

Anthony saw the speculation in his friend's gaze, but also the respect of his privacy. "Thank you, my friend, for hastening to inform me. I will not soon forget your support. Now, I must speak with Sebastian and then find Phillipa. I must not delay."

Anthony froze at Calvert's sudden stillness.

"Miss Phillipa Peppiwell?" he asked.

"Yes, what of it?"

Calvert gave him the most curious stare. "Why do you want to speak with her?"

Both Sebastian and Anthony measured Calvert carefully. Anthony's heart stalled, wondering how Orwell had embroiled her in whatever schemes he had set in motion. "The lady and I have an understanding. I will be speaking to her father this afternoon. At least, I'd planned to. I shall, after sorting out this mess."

"Damnation." Calvert raked his hands through his too-long hair.

"What is it?" Anthony growled, fearing the worst. Had Orwell started rumors of Phillipa's abduction, as well?

"Lord Hoyt was at that investors' meeting. He announced to everyone there his imminent engagement to Miss Peppiwell."

Betrayal shafted his insides, and he fought against the emotions that swamped him.

The lady had every right to beg off, but he could not credit that she would do so in such a cowardly manner, without speaking to him first.

"There is more," Calvert said sympathetically. "My mother had morning callers, and I heard whispers that some of the ladies plan to give your sister, Constance, the cut direct."

The curses that came from Sebastian were some of the most virulent Anthony had ever heard. He struggled to keep a calm facade in the face of them and his own rage. "Thank you, my friend, for letting us know."

Calvert rose, shook his hand, and departed.

"I must go to Constance at once." Anthony's mind churned as he gathered the piles of paper from the report and shoved them into the file jacket. "You say she is with Mother?"

"I will come with you."

He looked into the hard, angry face of his brother, shocked at the offer. Sebastian had not spoken to their mother in over a decade. Anthony wagered now would not be the best time for that first meeting. "Not necessary. Constance knows you adore her. But I really need to speak with her first."

Anthony saw Sebastian's disapproval, but he gave a short nod. "So, you made Miss Peppiwell an offer, after all," Sebastian growled, addressing the matter Anthony had determined to avoid. It must wait until after he'd dealt with his sister.

"I sent a note to Sherring Cross to let you know." He dismissed the concern in his brother's gaze and fought against the rage at how easy she'd deserted him.

The first hint of rumors of his illegitimacy, and she'd crumbled? *Good God*. She had seemed so fearless, so disdainful of Society. He'd actually believed she would wed him even knowing he was a bastard. He had planned to tell her everything this afternoon, before speaking to her father. What a gullible fool he had been.

He turned his mind from his rioting thoughts and focused on Sebastian.

"Humboldt arrived with news that Lord Orwell's lackeys paid him a visit." Humboldt was their family lawyer, and a powerful man in his own right.

"Why?"

"Orwell wanted the papers father left. Humboldt refused, of course," Sebastian said.

Which explained why Newport's offices had been ransacked, and the papers forcibly taken from Anthony's own attorney instead.

The brass balls of Orwell stunned Anthony. "Lord Orwell is growing too bold." He relayed to Sebastian about Phillipa's abduction and his rescue of her and about Newport's break-in.

"The hell, you say!" Sebastian snapped in outrage.

Anthony pushed the report across the table toward him. "It's all here. There is no doubt who is responsible for spreading the details of my illegitimacy."

If possible, Sebastian went colder. "I will crush him," Sebastian swore.

Anthony laughed mirthlessly. "You will need to get in line. Unfortunately, he has closed his houses and fled. He was last seen boarding a ship for the Continent."

"The bloody coward."

Anthony blew out a long, long, calming breath. "I find that I am more affected by Phillipa's desertion than Society learning I am a bastard," he said, meeting Sebastian's gaze unflinchingly. It took a hell of a lot to admit that.

"You love her?"

Anthony filled his glass with more port. "It is not like you to talk of love. I thought you did not believe in the notion."

"I do not believe in it for myself. That doesn't mean I don't want you to find love," Sebastian growled.

Anthony nodded. His brother had endured a bitter betrayal at the hands of a woman who'd claimed she adored him, so he could understand his cynicism. "I do love her. She is intelligent and passionate and finds the whirl of the *haute monde* tedious, the people lacking sincerity. Sentiments I agree with. However, it seems the lady has fallen prey to those same faults." The words tasted bitter.

"What will you do?"

He lifted a shoulder. "What is there to be done? The lady has made her choice." Though he tried to sound casual, the pain of her decision tied him in knots. He never dreamed he could feel such chaotic emotions over a female. "I think you may have the right of it brother. Women are not to be trusted," he said dispassionately.

Sebastian hesitated before he spoke. "I can see you closing off your emotions, just as you did when Father shut you out. If you love Miss Peppiwell as you say, then speak with her. Make her tell you to your face."

Anthony winced. Probably he was being spineless, but he feared what he might do if she admitted throwing him over for another man. The passion they burned with, the connection that had sparked between them…it hurt to think she could dismiss it all so callously. Over something she professed to disdain.

"I will not think on her one moment more," he vowed. "She never wanted to marry me in the first place. I will be damned if I profess love for her, trying to convince her not to marry Hoyt. He is welcome to the fickle chit."

Even as he said it, his gut turned to acid at the thought of her in Hoyt's arms, yielding to his embrace with the fire Anthony knew she possessed.

"I am more worried about Constance," he went on. "I cannot credit anyone would give her the cut without proof. But if Calvert is right—"

Sebastian muttered another curse. "Indeed, there is much to be done. We must protect Constance at all cost. But first you must call on your lady. I have never known you to be a coward, Anthony. Never. Speak with her before you make a decision that will haunt you for the rest of your life." Sebastian got to his feet, clasped his shoulder, and left him.

Anthony was so wrapped in his thoughts it took him a few moments to realize the gentlemen he normally drank and conversed with were treating him to covert glances. A sad smile curled his lips. Fickle, indeed. He looked up as a shadow loomed over him. It was Sebastian returning. Anthony arched a brow.

"It occurred to me that you may lack transportation. I will leave my carriage at your disposal. I have informed the coachman."

"I couldn't possibly impose," Anthony drawled, empting his glass of port, enjoying the warmth that trailed from his throat to stomach. "You'll need it to get back to Sherring Cross."

"Don't be an idiot," Sebastian snapped. "Deliver me to your town house and I will order up a traveling coach that's far more comfortable."

"Very well. Who am I to argue?" *No one, that was who.*

Anthony got to his feet, collected his greatcoat, and walked Sebastian out of the club they'd been members of for most of their lives—and their father before them, and his father before that. This would probably be the last time Anthony would be able to set foot in the establishment. Strangely, he discovered he cared not one whit.

What he cared about was confronting Phillipa. *Hell.* Going to her, to see the truth of her betrayal, was the hardest thing he would ever face. For, he realized he loved her unreservedly, and he'd never felt happiness as he had when she'd finally consented to marry him.

The future had seemed brighter. Dreams and promises had seemed possible.

How swiftly all his hopes had been swept away by bleak despair.

Chapter Sixteen

He had a sister to comfort.

And a father to confront.

Anthony shifted on his feet in front of Viscount Radcliffe's town house on St. James Street. He had been shivering outside in the cold for over five minutes, numbing himself to the surge of emotions that filled him. He was standing in front of his father's house.

His *real* father.

The knowledge settled in his stomach like lead. He and Radcliffe had never acknowledged each other as anything other than acquaintances and his mother's second husband. He had avoided the viscount in the days since learning of his true parentage, not knowing how to handle their first official meeting as father and son.

The old duke had died several years ago and his mother had wasted no time marrying the viscount, her long-time lover. Unlike Sebastian, Anthony had been happy for her, hating the shadows that had haunted her eyes all her life up until then. He had not judged her for not honoring a two-year mourning period for a man he had never seen her touch in all his years. But never had he imagined that Viscount Radcliffe was his and Constance's father. The man must surely have known the truth. But never had he revealed a hint of it to Anthony.

Not that he should have had to. Now that he knew, Anthony had only to look in a mirror to note the resemblance…and soon it would trumpet itself to the world.

He straightened his shoulders, climbed the steps with measured steps, and rapped on the door. The butler opened immediately, and Anthony could see the knowledge in his eyes. No surprise. Servants always knew everything before the masters of the house.

"No need to announce me," Anthony said. The clock in the foyer struck one o'clock as he stepped inside and handed him his things.

The haunting strains of a violin filtered through the air, and he followed them to Constance in the music room. She sat on a bench facing the windows with her back turned to him as she played. Her taut spine and the stiff manner in which she cradled the violin to her left cheek bespoke her emotions. She wore a plain blue day gown, with her mass of blond hair tumbling unfettered to her waist. He glanced down and saw her stockinged feet peeking out from under the hem of her dress.

"Constance." Anthony did not know how to face her. What to say to her.

She stiffened even further, but she did not pause. The violin cried with notes of such beauty his heart ached. He had never heard her play so poignantly before. When the last note dwindled he was regretful it ended. With reverent care, she stood and walked to its spindle and rested the violin and stick. She turned to him. Her tear-streaked face gutted him. Her gaze roamed his face as if she had never seen him before. He desperately wished he had never been so stupid as to wish for her to hold onto her childlike trust of the world. He should have told her at once. She should never have found out through cruel whispers.

"So, it is true." Her voice was hoarse and he knew that only happened after a long bout of crying.

"Yes."

She flinched as if struck, but he would give her nothing but the truth.

Where was their mother? Why was she not here comforting her daughter?

"You knew?" Constance asked.

"I learned a couple weeks ago. I was stupid not to tell you right away. I never dreamed it would come to this so quickly."

She nodded, tears trickling down her face. She hugged herself tightly, hunching into herself. "Why do you think mother never told us? Fath— The old duke hated me…hated us. And she made us think we were his children, Anthony."

He was not sure how to respond. He had asked himself the same question. He realized how different they would have seen themselves if they had known they were bastards. But still, they would not have been nearly as hurt by the old man's disdain had they understood the reason. And perhaps…they might have had a closer relationship with their real father.

"I do not excuse Mother's actions, Connie. And I know it may take time to forgive her and the viscount. But I think, in the end, she kept the knowledge to herself to protect us. To protect you from situations like the one you experienced today."

She wiped her face. "But how is it even possible? She was married!"

Good Lord. The girl was a true innocent. Realizing just how much so, he walked over and pulled her into his arms. Soft sobs shook her.

"Our mother made decisions we may never understand, Connie, but we must accept, and somehow live with them. I'm not saying it will be easy, but you mustn't be afraid. We will get through it. Together."

He led her from the music room toward the parlor. He saw his mother sitting on the staircase, her face in her hands, tears streaming down her cheeks. She glanced up and gave him a tremulous look.

He sighed, and managed a smile of reassurance.

Their mother had not been comforting Constance because she needed comforting herself. His heart warmed when he saw the viscount behind her, his arm around her shoulders in support.

Their eyes met, and Anthony wondered how he could have been so damned blind. They shared the same emerald-green eyes. The viscount's hair was turning lighter with age, but it was easy to see remnants of the golden blond it had once been, just like his own.

It struck Anthony that perhaps he had chosen to be blind all his life.

His mother rose, and they all entered the parlor and sank into the sofas. The viscount called for tea.

"You missed Miss Peppiwell's birthday celebration," Constance managed, though her voice was soft and hoarse. "Mother— Mother and I like her very much. Why weren't you there?"

He glanced at her, startled at the choice of subject. The last person he wanted to be thinking about was Phillipa. But Constance's lips were pinched, and he saw the need in her eyes to talk about something else.

"I… I had other things to attend to. I saw her afterward, at Lady Prescott's soiree."

"You got her a gift, then?"

"Yes. Last week." When he hadn't been able to stop

thinking about her.

"What did you give her? Diamonds, pearls, rubies? I think rubies would be marvelous with her red hair."

He chuckled softly and smiled. "I got her a map."

Constance lifted her head from where it had been resting on his shoulder to give him an appalled look. "A *map*? Are you mad?"

"She wants to travel the world. I thought she would love it. Though, I confess, I have yet to give it to her."

"Are you going to marry Miss Peppiwell?" his mother asked quietly.

He struggled through the feelings the question roused in him. "I, uh… I was going to. It appears… Things may have changed."

His sister's brow furrowed. "I suppose everything will be different now that we have been ostracized from society."

Their mother let out a sob and buried her face again. The viscount's expression had not wavered from anxious concern the whole time. His eyes met Anthony's again as he gathered his wife in his arms. "There, there," he murmured soothingly. "It will be all right, you'll see."

Anthony suddenly knew the man would do anything in the world to ease her pain and distress. His heart squeezed and his respect soared. How powerless Radcliffe must have felt all these years, loving a woman he could not have, and two children he could not raise, or even acknowledge.

Anthony resolved in his heart to try and be a true son to his father, if he'd let him. Somehow, he knew he would.

Constance slipped her hands into his, threading their fingers together. "What are we to do, brother?"

He sighed deeply. "You will go about as if everything is normal, and let me, Sebastian, and the viscount deal with it. When the season starts in the spring, you will attend all balls you are invited to, go on picnics, and take carriage rides. Then you will marry your prince charming."

Their mother looked up with a watery smile.

Constance frowned at him. "What do you know about my prince charming?"

"It's not as if you've kept it a secret that's what you desire."

He laughed at her indignant expression and tugged her back into his side. "You will be fine. True, things may be a bit different. But we do not care a fig about the eyes of Society, do we? What we care about is our family. And the friends who stand behind us. That is the most important thing we should all do, stick together, and remember we are a family, even if we are a complicated family."

The viscount smiled at him, then, and murmured, "Amen, son."

They were silent for the longest time, all of them staring into the crackling flame in the hearth, deep in their own thoughts.

"Anthony…" Constance ventured at length. "Why are you no longer considering Miss Peppiwell?"

His heart stalled. He continued to gaze into the fire, unable to see the pity in their eyes when he said, "It is the other way around, I'm afraid. I have heard Lord Hoyt has declared for her."

Constance gasped softly. "Are you certain?"

"Of his intentions? Yes. Of hers? I have not heard otherwise."

"Oh, darling. What are you going to do?" his mother asked.

He finally looked up. "What do you think I should do?"

She seemed to search his soul in the brief moment she considered him, but it was the viscount who quietly answered, "If you love her and cannot live without her, fight for her." A lifetime of regret lived in those words.

Constance gripped his hand. "He is right, Anthony. You

must not let another man steal her away from you."

Hell. His sister was very naive when it came to love. But Sebastian's advice resonated in his mind, along with the viscount's life lesson.

"Will you go to her? Ask who she's chosen?" his mother asked.

He nodded. He'd already made the decision to confront her. "Yes. I'd planned to speak to her father this afternoon, anyway. May as well keep that appointment." He needed to hear her rejection from her own lips.

That way, he could cut her from his heart completely, instead of spending a lifetime wondering.

...

Astonishment froze the crowd of callers who'd gathered in the Peppiwell's parlor when the butler announced Anthony, and he strolled in.

Phillipa's heart leaped, but her feet stayed anchored to the carpet.

She had been appalled by the number of callers who had shown up at their door today—"friends" who'd wanted to be sure she'd heard the scandalous news about her "admirer." Lord Hoyt, of course, had parked himself next to her and refused to budge. Phillipa had desperately wanted to flee the house, but her mother and aunt, and even her father, had all but imprisoned her and forced her to listen to the gossips speak ill of Anthony and his sweet sister. She held herself cold and detached, impervious to the malice surrounding her.

A high-pitched laugh from her mother cut off instantly upon seeing Anthony enter.

The crowd rippled away as he crossed the room toward Phillipa. They parted for him, both aghast and titillated by the dangerous glitter in his emerald eyes. Speculative stares darted between her and Anthony, and she hardened herself against the condemnation in their faces.

The look in Anthony's eyes shredded her, nearly shattering the icy composure she was determined to hide behind. Dressed in a dark gray coat and trousers with a peach waistcoat, he had never been more handsome.

"How did he get in?" Lady Merryweather said to her father in a loud whisper that everyone could hear. "Tell him to leave at once."

Anthony stopped in front of Phillipa, and her heart thundered.

"Introduce me to your fiancé." His voice was so smooth and toneless, completely at odds with the storm that swirled in his gaze.

She hardly knew how to respond. He was wrong. She had never accepted Hoyt. She was twenty-one now, and had already made plans to leave London. If she couldn't have Anthony, she wanted no other man. "I'm—"

"Come, my love, I do not wish to be introduced to an imposter," Lord Hoyt murmured caustically and took her arm.

Pain screamed inside her as Anthony went deathly still.

"He has some nerve coming here." The harsh whisper of Lady Jeffreys stabbed at her like a thousand knives. Anthony did not acknowledge any of the nasty comments as he waited for Phillipa's reaction.

Her mother threw her a horrified look. Her aunt's expression condemned from the far corner. Phillipa struggled for breath as she found herself standing all alone in the middle of the biggest crush her parlor had ever held. It seemed like all London society was watching her in keen anticipation. For her downfall, no doubt.

"Phillipa?" Anthony's low murmur raked over something deep inside her.

Expectation pressed in on her from her whole family. She could see the pleading in Payton's gaze.

Phillipa's mouth worked, but no sound came out. She gazed blindly at the hand Anthony held out to her. *Why would he come here? Why would he do this to me?* He must know she had no choice but to cut him. To save her family. Her eyes filled with tears as she forced herself to turn away without acknowledging him. She prayed he would give her a chance to explain later.

The relief in her sister's and mother's gazes condemned her, even as it freed them. The proud tilt of Hoyt's lips was unbearable. He squeezed her arm in reassurance, and she yanked it away from him.

Suddenly, Lady Henrietta gave a loud squeal of indignation. In her hand she held open the evening *Gazette*, which must have just been delivered. "How can this be?" she cried. "There is an announcement here, of Miss Peppiwell's imminent marriage to Lord Anthony!"

Every person in the room gasped. Every eye turned to Phillipa.

Phillipa could not help it…she glanced back at Anthony. His eyes went narrow and cold. His cynical look of utter disgust froze her to the spot. Hoyt took her arm again and tugged none too gently.

"Obviously, it is not true," Hoyt said loudly. "A vicious lie by the rogue to entrap an innocent lady."

She swallowed, unable to speak. She'd forgotten about the announcement Anthony had said he would send out.

A coldness chilled her to the bone when Anthony's lips curled up and icy contempt poured over her. "Obviously," he drawled.

Her heart cracked.

And then he dismissed her. She saw the moment he removed her from his thoughts and his heart…and her whole being shattered. She pulled herself from Hoyt's grasp and turned around fully to watch Anthony's retreat. The entire room watched her in morbid fascination, but she could not summon an ounce of energy to care. She gazed at his retreating back with a sickening sensation that blanched the blood from her face.

"Get hold of yourself, Phillipa," her mother softly hissed in her ear.

The crowd tittered drunkenly, smelling blood in the air. The murmuring began, and rose in an excited swell, that Phillipa Peppiwell had cut the bastard who'd dared to lie about their betrothal. She strained to see him stride through the crowd, ignoring the frantic pull of her mother and the harsh curses of Lord Hoyt.

"You are disgracing us, Phillipa," her aunt snapped, fanning herself with vigor.

The pain of loss that hazed Phillipa's mind pressed in on her, choking her, and suddenly she knew with every nerve of her body that she could not let him leave. She met her father's eyes then, and he smiled at her. A single tender smile of loving acceptance in a churning sea of disapproval. *Oh, Papa*.

She ripped away from everyone, ignoring the cries of the rest of her family to stop. She tried to press through to Anthony, but the crush of visitors slowed her down. Desperation clawed at her as she watched him reach the front entry and accept his coat from the butler, not looking back. Not knowing that she was trying to get to him.

He would be out the door and away in his carriage before she reached the foyer.

"Anthony!" she cried.

A startled hush fell over the parlor. He didn't turn. He didn't even slow, apparently uncaring that she was making a fool of herself. From the corner of her eye she saw her mother dip into a swoon, caught by Lord Hoyt.

Phillipa called even louder. "I love you, Anthony Thornton, and I don't give a goddamn who your father is!"

Her audacious declaration rang through the house, fierce and proud. She loved him, and she didn't care who knew. She wanted the whole world to know! And after this, it clearly would.

Fire scalded her cheeks as she waited anxiously for his reaction. The crowd parted between them like the Red Sea, holding its collective breath.

At last he halted, halfway through the front door.

Her heart surged with hope.

He turned with infinite grace, filling the other end of the ever-widening gap with his towering body and broad shoulders.

His response finally came in a slow, sensual smile. He captured her gaze and held it. This time, she did not hesitate when he held out his hands. She ran to him and placed her trembling hands in his.

"I love you," she said. "I care not what your name is, as long as I can share it."

His low laughter echoed through her, warm and comforting. He dipped his head and skimmed his lips over hers. There was a gasp of outrage from someone nearby, a startled laugh, and a fit of coughing. A lady swooned.

Anthony turned and walked out of the house, and she went willingly with him, her arm around his waist.

Her heart raced at her own daring. She could imagine the uproar that was going on behind her in the parlor, but she no longer cared. Her heart trembled. The look on her mother's and sister's faces had flooded her with guilt, but Anthony's shattered look had shredded her to ribbons. She gripped him tighter, the trembling of her body growing more pronounced.

The Calydon carriage waited at the curb, and he swept her inside, giving orders to the footman she could not decipher. The plush elegance of the interior did little to sooth her nerves as the coach rambled off with speed. He pulled down the blinds over the carriage's windows and shut out the world around them.

Then he looked over at her, his eyes glowed with an intensity she had never seen before. Not even when he had made love to her. Her eyes widened as he shrugged out of his coat and started to unbutton his waistcoat. Heat pooled inside her at the stark sensuality in his face.

"Where are we going, Anthony?" Her voice came out husky, filled with part fear and part excitement.

"To Gretna Green."

She blinked. Then her mouth split in a joyous smile, her composure completely rattled. But she felt reassured in a good way, a very good way. "To get married?"

"I thought you would like another adventure. We will be husband and wife. After all, the notification was in the *Gazette* and the *Times*, so it must be true."

"Indeed, it must," she agreed, and then she launched herself onto his lap and kissed him. "And I do like adventures."

He laughed under her loving attack. "I have a special license in my pocket. We can have a vicar marry us before we reach Scotland, or we can marry over a blacksmith's anvil."

"I like the anvil," she said in between kisses.

His hands tightened on her hips. "God, how I want you. You are my obsession."

She could feel the evidence of the desire that surged through him at her happy surrender. "Then take me, my lord."

He kissed her back, letting all his emotions and his passion pour over her like molten honey. After a long, thorough kiss, she gifted him with the most radiant smile she had ever felt.

"We will travel together," she said. "Sail the oceans, and be free."

"We can visit wherever you wish, for as long as you want.

I have enough wealth to take us on a thousand adventures," he murmured. "I want only to please you."

Her heart was dizzy with elation. "Does this mean you love me, my lord?"

"It means I love and adore you completely."

...

Everything that had ever been cold in Phillipa melted. A sensual smile curved her lips and heat seeped through her. The carriage jostled and rumbled over the streets and complete happiness unfurled within her.

"I meant what I said earlier," she said. "But are the rumors true?"

He nodded unflinchingly. "Yes, my father is the Viscount Radcliffe. This untimely revelation is Orwell's doing. He has attempted to exact vengeance on us for foiling his plans to have you."

Phillipa listened aghast as he told of the old duke's letter and the break-in at his solicitor's office. Pain sliced her at the unfairness. "I am so sorry, Anthony. You and your sister were hurt because of me."

He scowled. "The fault lies with Orwell, not you. Don't ever say this is your fault, for it is not." His gaze was resolute.

Her eyes widened and she nodded. "I promise."

"Do you trust me, Phillipa?"

A subtle tension swirled around them. Her heart stuttered. She wished only to be held in his arms. "Yes, more than I have ever trusted anyone."

He nodded, and the coiled tension eased. "My brother and I, and the viscount, will deal with Orwell and the repercussion of the scandal. You and I shall leave London, I promise, Phillipa. However, we must stay for a little while first. For the sake of my sister Constance and for that of your family. The gossips will devastate our dear sisters, society will crush them, and their dreams will be shattered unless we stem the tide of condemnation before it takes them under."

Phillipa's throat tightened. "I am so sorry you and Constance will be judged by circumstances that do not measure your worth as the honorable man I know you are, or the wonderful lady that she is."

"Thank you."

"Your father, the late duke…" Questions twisted in her, but the flare of hurt in his eyes halted them. Her heart ached for him. "Why did he do this?"

Anthony hesitated. "I doubt I will ever know for sure. I suppose at the end he despised the very thought of me ever inheriting his estates. In any case, a large part of me is glad he was not my real father. He was never a true father to me. But pray, let us talk of anything but this."

She wanted to throw herself into another kiss with him, yet hesitated at the slightly guarded look in his eyes.

"So…you adore me?" she murmured, dropping her voice to a husky whisper.

The guarded look was replaced by a slow, devastating smile. "With a depth you cannot comprehend."

A thrill surged through her. She wanted to vanquish his hurt and pain, to soothe his turmoil. She moved her leg over his thighs to straddle his lap. Slanting him a coy look, she drew her skirts up her legs, as far as they would go.

A strangled groan escaped from his lips as she bared herself to his gaze. She had left her drawers off again, so she widened her legs lasciviously.

"I see you waste no time behaving scandalously," he growled, his eyes glowing with lust and intense love.

She waggled her brows, and laughed as he drew her over himself. The emotions roiling in his eyes sent shivers through her. Need flowered in her and she grew moist from desire.

With efficient movements he freed himself and notched the broad head of his erection at her entrance. There was no need for foreplay. His hands clasped her buttocks and with a powerful surge he embedded himself within her.

He captured her cry. "I love you, Miss Peppiwell. Scandal will follow us all our lives, I wager. But to experience your indomitable spirit, your passion, and sensuality, and the love I can see so clearly in your eyes, is more than enough to fill a lifetime without a single regret."

She nodded as his hands on her buttocks tightened, lifted her, and with a forceful movement, which had her crying out urged her down on him to meet his upward thrust. "You will never be bored with me, either," he vowed. "I will introduce you to sexual pleasures you could not have imagined. You will always be free and loved for your daring and your passion," he promised, voice rough with emotions.

He captured her lips with a kiss so full of wild, aching hunger she felt it to her very soul. Bliss seared her and she returned his kiss with all the love and hunger within her.

"You fill my dreams, meet my needs, and soothe my fears. I love you, Anthony," she whispered against his lips, shivering under the rush of exquisite pleasure.

Their pleasure burned bright into the carriage that jostled them toward their first adventure, to become husband and wife.

She pushed away her doubts and accepted the love he had to give, as they raced toward an uncertain but thrilling future.

Chapter Seventeen

The cold that penetrated the walls of Castle Kildern could not dampened Phillipa's spirits. She was now married in truth to Anthony, and she had never been happier.

Their honeymoon thus far had been an exciting experience. Every night, over the past two weeks, Anthony had taken her to sexual heights that caused her even now to blush. Their days of talking and touring several ancient castles in the southwest of England drew her more and more into his life and his past. She'd come to realize how much of himself he had hidden behind the charming rogue he presented to the world. The pain in his eyes was deep when he spoke of the man he thought had been his father and the isolation and criticism he had endured at his hands. Thankfully, their blossoming relationship with his mother and his real father, Lord Radcliffe, more than made up for the past and brought joy to all their lives.

Phillipa had seen the strength and kindness of her new husband's character more each day, and she had not though it possible to be more besotted with him. Then, the week after their hasty marriage, he'd given her his belated birthday gift. A map. And he'd told her all she needed to do was mark each spot she would like to visit, and he would add it to their upcoming Grand Tour. She had been humbled, delighted, and had hugged him for unending minutes.

But now they were indulging a short, secret honeymoon, a calming respite before returning to London.

"I can hardly credit that two weeks ago I stood in my parents' parlor terrified they would announce my engagement to Lord Hoyt, and now I am your wife," Phillipa murmured contentedly.

Anthony grunted. "I do not think it wise to remind me that you were engaged to another man."

"I wasn't! I told you I'd planned on refuting their claims if they had made an announcement." She laughed and rolled out of his arms, drawing on the silk dressing gown resting on a peg by the bed.

Castle Kildern and the southwest of England were among the most beautiful places she'd ever seen. She loved the dense forest that surrounded the valleys, and she could feel the rich history of the castle to her very bones.

"Must we travel back today?" she asked as she performed her ablutions. She buried the unease she felt over her imminent return to her family. Over having to face Payton, to whom she had written and received no reply. Their rush to Gretna Green, being married, returning to Anthony's castle briefly, and then their secret honeymoon days and nights of tumultuous loving, reading together, playing piquet and chess had erased everything else from her mind. Now the fantasy was coming to an end, and it was hard not to worry about the difficult reality of what lay ahead.

"We must. I have informed both our families of our whereabouts, but we can no longer delay our return to London. A couple days ago the *Gazette* published the notice that our wedding will take place in a few weeks. You must go back to your parents until that time and plan your trousseau. Though it is fairly certain few have truly been fooled by your pretense of rusticating in Dorset with your mother's cousin, in the official eyes of society we are not yet married. You must act the part of eager bride, for your family's sake, at least."

She sighed gustily and leaned into the heat that came up behind her. He spun her gently around, dipped his head, and captured her lips in a soothing kiss.

"Let's hope, with you tucked away and me supposedly in Baybrook preparing for my new bride, that Society has moved on to more interesting tittle-tattle for their prying eyes and wagging tongues."

"Have you heard anything of Orwell?"

"He has fled, as we suspected. My agents will not miss his return to London, if he ever dares."

She twined her hands around Anthony's neck and tipped up, claiming another kiss.

She broke away long moments later. "I love you so much, my husband." She doubted she would ever tire of telling him that, or of the sensual smile that curved his mouth each time she whispered the words.

"I love you, too, my sweet." He pressed another soft kiss to her lips. "Let us ring for breakfast and prepare for our journey."

"Yes. We should do that," she murmured. But instead, she deepened the kiss and moaned softly, getting lost in the pleasures his body bestowed.

With a throaty chuckle, he walked her backward toward the bed, and she smiled.

Breaking their fast could wait a while longer.

...

Distracted by the sensual way Phillipa ate her croissant after they'd made love, it took Anthony three readings for the short notice in the *Times* to make any sense to him. And even then, it made no sense at all.

"Good God!" he finally exclaimed, nearly dropping his coffee cup.

Phillipa glanced up at his outburst. She lowered her fork and gave him a quizzical look. "What is it?"

With a feeling of complete and utter astonishment, he read the notice aloud to her, still unable to credit the meaning.

"Lord Sebastian Thornton, the Twelfth Duke of Calydon, announces his marriage to Lady Jocelyn Rathbourne."

Phillipa's jaw dropped. "Good heavens. I had no idea he was betrothed. Is this the Lady Jocelyn you told me about? The one you gave your mother's locket?"

He looked at Phillipa, wondering if hell had frozen over. Or perhaps he'd somehow entered one of Jules Verne's fantastical worlds. Sebastian *married*? To *Jocelyn*? "Yes. It is she."

"I wasn't aware they knew each other."

"They don't." Anthony read the notice for the fifth time. "This must be a joke. Some kind of prank. Sebastian does not believe in marriage. He vowed never to wed." She scraped back her chair and moved to read the notice over his shoulder. "I doubt the *Times* would print such a serious announcement unless it came from the duke himself."

He nodded slowly. "You are right, of course. But still… I just can't believe it."

Sebastian married? He thought about Lady Jocelyn's fiery temperament and his brother's infinite coldness and bitterness toward women. *Good God*. It was a disaster in the making, if ever there was one.

"The good news is," he mused, "this development will certainly divert the attention of Society from us…and hopefully from my parentage, as well. Now that I may in due course cease to be Sebastian's heir." He suddenly smiled broadly. "Why, the dirty scoundrel!" Anthony murmured gleefully. "He's gotten her with child. That must be the explanation!"

"What will you do?" Phillipa asked, giving him a curious grin.

He laughed incredulously, put the paper down, and pulled her into his lap. "Do? Not a damned thing, other than send a note of hearty congratulations." He grimaced anew. "From as great a distance away as possible. Knowing both Jocelyn and Sebastian, the best strategy is to stay far away from the fireworks."

Phillipa giggled. "Surely, the situation can't be *that* explosive."

"No, perhaps not," he said wryly. "I'd wager that it is volcanic!"

He laughed at her astonishment. He loved the way her eyes sparkled with mischief. He would never tire of looking at her, of kissing her, of just being near her.

"Now you have me really curious. We must call on them."

"Just a few weeks before Christmas? Constance and I normally spend the holiday at Sherring Cross. We will see them then." He exhaled. "But for now, you must return to your parents, and I will speak with your father."

She arched her brows, amused. "So, after you have compromised me thoroughly, whisked me away and married me. Kept me secluded in this castle fortress for two weeks… *Then* you're going to speak with my father?"

The glitter in her eyes slowly dimmed.

He searched her countenance. "Why are you worried? He's already given us his blessing, my sweet. Both the night of our elopement, and since, in our correspondence."

She dropped her forehead against his and sighed. "It's not

him. I...I've heard nothing from Payton, and I am sure she received all five letters from me. If I have any regrets for my actions that night, it would be how they affected Payton. She truly loves Jensen St. John, and I may have made a muck of things for her."

Anthony thought about everything he knew about the Jensen boy. Intelligent, eager, a little hotheaded at times, but honorable. "If he loves her, Phillipa, he will stand by her. I will speak with him."

"Would you? Oh, thank you."

He kissed her tenderly, wishing he could promise all would be well. But he had learned over the years life was everything but certain or fair.

The only thing of which he was certain was his deep, abiding love for his new wife. He would always do everything in his power to keep her healthy and happy. And knew she would do the same for him.

...

Anthony had been away from Phillipa for a little over two weeks, and it was hell. He'd taken her back to her family and spoken with her father. Mr. Jonas Peppiwell was smart and obviously possessed a grand vision for his family's future. But he was also a puritanical, social-climbing prig. Anthony had met his sort before and despised their unbending espousal of lofty values with no thought to circumstance.

He had wanted to plant a fist in Mr. Peppiwell's face when he had stated his daughter was soiled goods, and that he was immensely grateful someone else would now have to deal with her strong will and unorthodox ways.

With most of the *haute monde* now retiring to the country for hunting, shooting, and the holidays, Anthony hoped he and Phillipa would be somewhat safe from the stultifying gaze of Society. He'd sworn to her aunt to keep his distance from her until they were safely—that is, publically—wed. No carriage rides, no evenings at the theater and absolutely no clandestine meetings. He'd agreed to set their wedding date for Boxing Day—the day after Christmas—at his newly renovated estate in Hampshire.

The wedding was to be an intimate ceremony followed by a small celebratory feast, with only family and close friends in attendance. His lips twisted cynically. Which wasn't a big problem, since his formerly vast stable of acquaintances had dwindled to a mere handful.

His close friends had already written to him expressing their sympathies, and although he had been blackballed by his clubs, he was unconcerned about being forced to leave them. He expected fewer invitations from the upper crust, but knew his real friends would be supportive.

With Christmas less than a week away, he'd received Sebastian's note informing him of his marriage, and also a formal invitation from the duchess to Christmas dinner. He'd also thought it best to greet the duchess now, not before a full gathering at Christmas dinner. He wondered if she'd told his brother of their…brief connection. Feeling more than awkward about it, he had yet to broach that topic with Sebastian.

They stood now in his brother's stately library, sharing a drink before the fire.

"Are you sure Constance is well?" Sebastian asked him for the third time.

Anthony sighed, and moved to inspect a new volume he spied on the bookshelf behind the door. "As well as can be expected. She is still at Lord Radcliffe's country home. She and Mother will return to London at the opening of the season. Connie is more than reluctant, but she's a brave little thing and will go along despite her fears."

Sebastian nodded grimly. "Lord Andrew Bellamy offered for her several weeks ago. He begged off, no doubt because of the rumors about her parentage."

"He is a dishonorable cad, then, and not worthy of her," Anthony snarled, snapping the book shut and replacing it.

Before Sebastian could reply, the door to the library swung open, nearly hitting him, and Lady Jocelyn sailed in. She was dressed in a pale pink tea gown with her hair swept high in an intricate knot.

She closed the door, clearly not aware Anthony was standing right behind her.

Sebastian asked politely, "How my I assist you, Jocelyn?"

"I am in love with you," she announced without preamble. She leaned against the closed door, her hands clasped tightly around the handle.

Astonished, Anthony started to step forward, but Sebastian gave him a quelling look and he remained rooted.

"I am in love with you, Sebastian," she continued agitatedly." I *love* you. Your warmth, your generosity with your tenants, your intensity…your passion. Your—"

"Enough, madam!" Sebastian bit out furiously, seeming even more astonished than Anthony.

Jocelyn, however, persisted, and the conversation grew even more intimate. Anthony was horrified. Both at his part in the scene, and at Sebastian. He had never heard his brother's voice so cold and forbidding as when he attempted to shut down his wife's declaration of love. Anthony wanted to punch his brother. She was laying her heart bare and he just sat there, unmoved.

Anthony's admiration for her soared when she did not back down, but soldiered on to outline exactly how things stood with her. But then he was not surprised, given her temperament.

When she was finished, she did not wait for his brother's

response, or even watch his reaction. She whirled, jerked the door open, and stalked from the room.

Anthony would have laughed at the look of shock that chased Sebastian's face—if the situation were not so damnably serious.

He cleared his throat. "I do not believe Jocelyn was aware that I was in the room."

"Whatever gave you that impression?" his brother ground out.

Despite the awkwardness, Anthony was inordinately pleased to see how rattled his normally unshakable brother was. Sebastian needed a good shaking up, and suddenly Anthony was damn glad the irrepressible Jocelyn Rathbourne had snared the duke, no matter how it had come about. "Never have I seen you looking quite so at a loss, Sebastian."

"Shut up, damn it." His brother sent him a deadly scowl, shot to his feet, and stalked to the drinks tray. "How is Phillipa?

Anthony raised his brow at the abrupt shift in topic. "Very happy and contented. She will journey down with her sisters and parents in a couple of days." He took a healthy swallow of his whiskey, not willing to let the matter go. He was dying of curiosity to find out how in damnation his marriage-phobic brother ended up in shackles. His note had only mentioned he'd acquired a duchess. "I thought someone was playing a prank when I read in the *Times* that you had wed Lady Jocelyn Rathbourne. Then I realized it must be true, because who would dare?"

His brother grunted and went to the windows. He opened them a crack, letting in the chill.

"Bloody hell, Sebastian, you and the damn cold!" Anthony rose and joined him, gazing out at the landscape that was blanketed white with snow. "How on earth did it come about that you married Lady Jocelyn?"

A muscle ticked in Sebastian's jaw. She'd obviously gotten

under Sebastian's skin. It was about damn time. After the debacle with his last mistress, he had been too alone for the last several years, deliberately closing off himself from female companionship.

"She barged into my study with a derringer, claiming you had taken advantage of her, and demanding satisfaction."

Anthony froze. "The hell, you say!"

Sebastian laughed. "She was quite amazing. So I thought instead of choosing one of the vapid, shallow misses who pepper the *ton*, I would prefer a bold and adventurous woman who is not afraid to speak her mind. Which, she certainly isn't," he added drily. "Although I've come to realize that my days would be far more peaceful with a more biddable wife."

They exchanged a look and both laughed.

"But not nearly as interesting, I wager." Anthony wondered if Sebastian saw how he came alive when he spoke of her.

He decided he should make a clean breast of it to his brother concerning his halfhearted pursuit of Lady Jocelyn. Anthony didn't want any doubts on Sebastian's part about how far things did or did not go between himself and the duchess. Just in case any of it played a role in that little scene moments ago. He concluded by explaining about the locket.

He felt Sebastian's glance and thoughtful nod, and they went on to speak of other things. He was grateful the topic of his illegitimacy did not come up again. Anthony did not want every conversation to center on that and what they would do about it. They settled into their easy camaraderie, their conversation only becoming tense when Anthony mentioned their mother. That was one subject Sebastian categorically refused to engage in. Anthony wondered if he would ever forgive her. He was pretty sure his brother's difficulty with love in all its forms stemmed from their mother's dishonorable treatment of his father.

But Anthony had forgiven their mother, and had always kept himself open to the idea of love and family. As a result, perhaps, he had found a perfect love with Phillipa. The laughter, the joy, the companionship, the trust, that was what made life worth living.

...

Christmas Day

Phillipa stood in the bracing cold of the garden, fingering the resilient petals of a bloodred winter rose that lingered on a snow-covered bush. Tomorrow she would wed Anthony again, but this time it would be properly in a church. Which would make their union respectable for all the world to see and criticize if they wished. She hoped the news of their nuptials would dampen some of the scandal swirling about them.

She had missed her husband fiercely in the days they had been apart. But she had also welcomed spending a little time with her family. Time to explain the details they weren't aware of. Time to heal their relationships.

Phillipa's mother and her aunt, Lady Merryweather, had quickly forgotten their vehement objections to her marrying Anthony when the Duke of Calydon had let it be known in no uncertain terms, that he fully supported his brother and would sever ties with anyone who dared to cut Anthony. However, Phillipa knew the true test would come when the *beau monde* returned to London for the season. Not being ostracized by Society was a vastly different thing than being embraced...or even accepted.

There was one bright note, though. Sebastian's sudden marriage meant that, with any luck, Anthony would soon be replaced as the duke's heir apparent. Thank God for that. Neither he nor Phillipa relished the weight of that responsibility, and were overjoyed at the welcome development.

Now she only needed to get through Christmas and the wedding. Then social obligations would be fulfilled, and she and her husband could go about the business of living their lives.

She lifted her head and glanced in through the windows of Sherring Cross as laughter spilled into the air. She smiled at the joyous sounds and shrieks from Lady Jocelyn's young brother and sisters, and her own sister, Phoebe, as they romped. Phillipa's entire family had traveled to the duke's country home for the holiday feast and the wedding. Constance and Anthony's mother and his true father, Lord Radcliffe, were also both present. It had been poignant watching the tentative and growing relationships of the new family emerge. Connections once hidden, and now highly unconventional, had wrought some awkward moments. But overall, nearly everyone seemed overjoyed at the possibilities for the future.

Lady Jocelyn's family was also present, her father and sisters and her brother. Phillipa liked them tremendously.

Laughter and joy had burned bright as they exchanged gifts on Christmas morning, played parlor games, and simply basked in each other's presence. Phillipa had never felt so content and hopeful.

"What on earth are you doing out here? It is too cold. You'll catch your death."

She shifted, her heart swelling with love as Anthony made his way into the garden. She gathered the small bouquet of red roses in her lap and held them up to her nose. "I cut these for Payton's room." She tilted her head toward the solarium, where her sister sat despondently. "Her heart is breaking."

He glanced toward Payton. "I wish there was something we could do or say to make things better for her." He sat beside Phillipa and drew her close.

She snuggled into his side, the vital heat radiating from his body warming her. "Lord St. John has not retracted his offer, but he is notably cooler. I am happy she does not blame me for the change in him. But if your parentage is the reason he is behaving so stupidly, then he values society's opinion more than he values Payton, and it's best she knows that now, before they are married. Still, I hurt for her."

Anthony's hand tightened around her shoulder. "He is young. It often takes some years of living to learn what true honor is all about." He glanced at her with an ironic smile. "And yet, the young are not the only ones so easily misguided by narrow-minded censure."

She sighed, glancing at her sister, aching for her. "Honor is a difficult lesson not everyone learns. I hope for her sake he comes to understand what is truly important in life."

"Either way, we will be here for her, and for Constance, until the scandal dies and is forgotten."

She nestled closer. "I pray you are right, and it all goes away." She doubted she would ever understand why Society was so hypocritical, condemning behavior that everyone ignored but knew was going on. As long as marriages were made for political reasons rather than for love, men and women would continue to pursue illicit alliances outside the marriage bed. To ostracize anyone for doing so was to deny the basic human need for love.

Speaking of which…

"Lady Jocelyn is lovely," she said with a smile. "And your brother…when he looks at her, I see they are the perfect match. We have that, too, don't we?"

"We do, my love."

"I so want Payton and Constance to find their perfect matches, as well."

"They will, you'll see. Just give them time."

He kissed her forehead, and contentment Phillipa had never known filled her whole being. "I do love you so."

He dipped his head and met her lips. "I'll spend my life

endeavoring to be worthy of that love."

"I have never doubted it. You are my heart, Anthony."

"And you are mine, my sweet wife."

She smiled and sent a prayer of thanks to the heavens that they had found each other. Her life before Anthony had been so dull and unfulfilled, with only a lifetime of restrictions and disappointments to look forward to.

Anthony promised her love and excitement and endless adventure. They would tour the four corners of the world together, free as the wind.

But she also knew, even if she never traveled more than a mile from home, she had already embarked upon the journey of a lifetime…for a lifetime. So far it promised unending delight, the grand adventure of being loved and cherished by Anthony Thornton.

And that was the best adventure of all.

Acknowledgments

This would not have been possible without the blessings and favour of God. To my husband Dusean, whom I adore. Thank you for being my biggest fan and supporter, and for loving the fact that I am a ninja in disguise.

To my amazing editor Nina Bruhns, for enjoying my characters as much as I do, being challenging yet supportive, and just fabulous to work with!

To Gwen Hayes who made me dig deeper for a sweeter hero in Anthony.

To historical romance author Giselle Marks, for being the most fabulous and thorough critique partner.

To my wonderful readers, thank you for picking up my book and giving me a chance! You guys rock!

Thank You!

About the Author

I am an avid reader of novels with a deep passion for writing. I especially love romance and adore writing about people falling in love. I live a lot in the worlds I create and I actively speak to my characters (out loud). I have a warrior way "never give up on my dream." When I am not writing, I spend a copious amount of time drooling over Rick Grimes from *Walking Dead*, watching Japanese Anime and playing video games with my love—Dusean Nelson. I have a horrible weakness for ice cream.

I am always happy to hear from readers and would love for you to connect with me via Website | Faceook | Twitter

To be the first to hear about my new releases, get cover reveals and excerpts you won't find anywhere else, sign up for my Newsletter, or join me in The Riot.

Happy reading!

Discover the **Scandalous House of Calydon** *series...*

THE DUKE'S SHOTGUN WEDDING

SINS OF A DUKE

THE ROYAL CONQUEST

Also by Stacy Reid

ACCIDENTALLY COMPROMISING THE DUKE

WICKED IN HIS ARMS

HOW TO MARRY A MARQUESS

Get Scandalous with these historical reads…

HIS LORDSHIP'S WILD HIGHLAND BRIDE
a *Those Magnificent Malverns* novel by Kathleen Bittner Roth

Ridley Malvern, Lord Caulfield, desperate for a dowry, agrees to marry a wealthy Scot's daughter sight unseen. All Lainie MacGregor desires is to return to her clan. Attempting to make things right, Caulfield takes Lainie back to the Highlands only to discover that his wife is wanted for murder. For her safekeeping, they must remain in England. Now Ridley needs to win her affections and prove that a wild Highland lass and an English lord, can find a love match, after all.

SEDUCING THE MARQUESS
a *Lords and Ladies in Love* novel by Callie Hutton

Richard, the Marquess of Devon is satisfied with his ton marriage. His wife of five months, Lady Eugenia Devon wants her very proper husband to fall in love with her. After finding a naughty book, she begins a campaign to change the rules. Her much changed and decidedly wicked behavior drives her husband to wonder if his perfect Lady has taken a lover. But the only man Eugenia wants is her husband. The book can bring sizzling desire to the marriage or cause an explosion.

The Duke's Obsession
by Frances Fowlkes

LONDON, 1818

Edward Lacey, the Duke of Waverly, finds American heiress Daphne Farrington delightful, despite her mysterious contempt towards him. He wants nothing more than to convince her that not all English lords are callous, calculating rakes. In fact, he can't seem to let go of the notion she might be the duchess he is looking for. But when he discovers that his family figures prominently in the cause of her bitterness, will he be able to overcome her pride and prejudice?

The Love Match
a *Sisters of Scandal* novella by Lily Maxton

Olivia Middleton prefers gothic novels to hunting for a husband. Only the charming and infuriating Mr. William Cross (a rake in the making, and certainly not a suitable husband) holds the slightest fascination for her. After watching his father die of a broken heart, William has sworn never to wed for a love match. Yet he's intrigued by the bookish Olivia. And though he tries, staying away from her turns out to be impossible.

Printed in Great Britain
by Amazon